The Garden of Magic and Witchcraft

By Shaya Motamedi

&

Mohammad Atashbarg

Inspired by Frances Hodgson Burnett's
«The Secret Garden»

Serial Number: P2515250270
Title: The Garden of Magic and Witchcraft
Language: Bilingual (Farsi - English)
Author: Shaya Motamedi
Translator: Mohammad Atashbarg
Illustrator: Mahboobeh
ISBN: 978-1-77892-276-3
Metadata: Junior Fiction, Mystery
Book Size: Paperback
Pages: 114
Publication Date: May 2026
Publisher: Kidsocado International Publishing Inc.

Kidsocado International Publishing Inc.
Vancouver, Canada

Phone & WhatsApp: +1 (236) 333-7248
Email: info@kidsocado.com
Website: https://kidsocado.com
Address: 2100-1055 West Georgia St,
Vancouver, BC V6E 3P3, Canada

For my mom,

This is my first book
which means my first pub-
lic dedication!
So, of course it had to be
you. I am beyond glad you
kept pushing me to do this
writing thing.

I love you <3

"All the king's horses and all
the king's men, couldn't put me
together again."

-Taylor Swift

PROLOGUE

You know that one thing people always say: "the hard days are what make you stronger." Well, I think whatever it is that I'm writing here, captures that sentence perfectly. No- that's a lie.

See how easy it was to fake being happy and strong? I know that people also say "fake it, till you make it," but I've been faking for such an interminably long time that I have seemingly forgotten how to show true, raw emotion.

As you can see, I am not well, so if I seem slightly asinine in some parts, gimme a break.

So, now that the introduction is out of the way, here is my tale, which is perfect for people like you. People who are hurting. Hurting on the inside. People who act like they are fine but have an anger inside them, just waiting to come out. Smiling, beaming in public, but going home to the sound proof walls of their bathrooms, crying, sobbing like they don't already do it everyday.

This story is not here to bring a message and say "everything is going to be okay."

Because it's not.

Well, in my case it wasn't.

You'll see.

Chapter 1

The air was cold.......

The air was cold. There I was, crouched behind the white SUV, looking up slowly. There they were, my mother, younger sister Sabrina, and my older brother Toby, lying on the side of the road, blood flowing freely everywhere. I wished greatly that I could rush over to them and cry until no more tears came out. But she was still there. Knife in hand, slowly pacing back and forth with a grin on her chalk-pale face. Time seemed to stop. Everything seemed to be quiet.

Until I heard my mother's voice.

"You need to be careful Maya, you are her. <u>Her.</u> You are....."

She didn't have time to finish her sentence and now

she never will.

I lay on my belly behind the car, stomach twisting and aching with every breath I took. I was shaking, my heart nearly beating out of my chest, pushing against my rib cage. I wanted to lay here and cry; instead, I pushed down that guilt and fear.

I tried to reach for my phone. A shadow moved in the corner of my eye. The sound of a knife falling to the ground pierced through the air. Soon, I was face to face with a creepy figure, her icy blue eyes shining through the darkness.

She let out a laugh.

I woke up with a start, sweat dripping down my face, pooling into my tired eyes.

I have been having that exact dream for the past year and I can't seem to move on. My body aches from the lack of peaceful sleep. "This is your life. It has been for the past year, so get up and try to move on, like you *always* do." I

told myself confidently.

I practically tripped down the long-marbled staircase for breakfast, passing all the empty-rooms. I passed the only room in the house locked with three locks, except two locks were opened and the keys were on the green carpet before it. I was intrigued, but had no choice but to go quickly down for breakfast. Uncle Brian was making French toast and scrambled eggs. My stomach churned at his kindness. I never talk to him, and I feel bad about it. He has never done anything to me, but I don't feel anything enough to have a completely normal interaction with him.

I ate quickly and got ready for school. I should not have to go to school after this whole thing. It's not fair having to lock myself in the girls' washroom everyday just so I could let out my tears. It stings so much to think about it. To think about them. Their pained expressions before their hearts gave out. The way my mother could almost reach out and touch my cheek as I sat with them, sobbing with my head in my bloody hands.

No one could know how it feels being in this state of melancholia.

And it's not like I would tell them.

I cuddled with my dog, Hazel, for a bit before leaving. I took a deep breath as I exited through the door and out into the sunny day.

The grass was green, the sky was blue; the children laughed and ran through the streets, but I couldn't dare to look at them. It brought me memories, sweet memories of my old life.

That only brought me pain.

So, I pushed the thought even further away, until it was shoved far in the back of my mind.

For the whole day I did everything as I should and avoided Evie, my old best friend. Because if it wasn't for the fight that she started, I would have gone outside with my family.

Sometimes I like to think that I somehow cheated death because of that, but it doesn't really help the fact that I am all alone, with the exception of Hazel, my dog, who I am glad

survived with me. I avoided everyone. It's not like anyone actually cares if I talk to them. They all seem to either feel sad for me in a sarcastic way, not care, or think that I made it up. Not a lot of people have their whole families get stabbed to death on a road trip.

As soon as I got home, I made myself my beloved NPB sandwich (AKA, Nutella, peanut butter, and bananas), and went to the door I had seen this morning. I picked up the key and opened the lock. The door opened and there was a pure white glow before me. I stepped in, letting my curiosity get the best of me. Hazel slid in with me. She's a pretty adventurous dog.

The room wasn't really a room it was more like a garden. A *secret garden*. I thought. *Like the book.* Although, I have never seen this garden from the front of the house, even though I could see the road in front of the house. Shocked by what I had come across in this 'room', I felt a small smile escape my lips. The grass was the greenest thing I had ever seen and there were flowers of all colours. When I looked up from the ground,

I could again see a bright flash of white in the sky, and just after, everything around me turned a neutral grey, even my clothes. I had on my favourite sweater, a maroon crewneck with dark blue baggy jeans. My short brown hair was down and was also turned grey. Even Hazel was grey. It was honestly sad seeing her in that state of dullness.

In the corner of my eye, I spotted a door covered with vines. The peculiar thing was, I was still grey, all around me was still grey, but that corner where that door lay, was the only colourful thing in the whole garden. I went over to the door and observed it more carefully. There was a single flower that wasn't found in the entire garden, a beautiful periwinkle coloured Lotus with tiny streaks of a vibrant green and blue.

As I curiously opened the wood door, a strong yellow glow overcame the garden and I fell to the ground nauseated.

The last thing I remember was being on the grass, where a creepy girl with blood all over

her was looking down at me. I closed my eyes to try to look away.

I couldn't help but scream.

"Oh, Maya, let's go get some air!" My mother called out ecstatically. I opened my eyes slowly and stared at the new environment, where, for some very odd reason, I could hear the sweet sound of my mother calling me. It's as if the accident never even happened. As if my own family was not brutally murdered right in front of me. *"Oh my gosh, Maya, just get out of your room we're going for a walk, gosh."* My brother said to me in his old funny voice. He also did his good old hand gesture where he snaps his wrist down. We laughed. My stomach cramped up. Laughing felt so odd now. I felt like even if I were dreaming, I would never feel this much happiness again, from the moment the murder happened. But I went along with whatever that was happening to me, and I got out of my room and went outside for a walk. The air still smelled

salty and the sky was still grey, like in the garden.

I started coughing, but no one came to help me. And suddenly, the idea of their death truly hit me. They were really gone and I was really, truly, alone. Hazel sat down beside me and all I could hear was the silence of my front yard.

Chapter 2

It was a normal day for the
abandoned...

It was a normal day for the abandoned tower where the deadliest creatures lived, and a semi-normal day for the horrible house right next to the tower, which had humans living in it.

Since the recent arrival of a beautiful girl with glowing eyes and the longest dress, the creatures were in hiding and the large garden around the tower was eerie and dead silent.

In the tower she lived in though, it was chaotic, fumy, and messy. There she was, sitting around the infamous Cauldron of Hell, where many creatures were enchanted, destroyed, and murdered. In her head lived an evil and mysterious plan. A plan that will eliminate those special people in this world.

This girl was a dangerous girl of mystery, Myera, her name coming from the last name *Myers*, simply meaning *evil*.

Police have tried to track her down, but it is impossible, as she is now nearly unstoppable, and the only one that could stop her was still clueless of how powerful they really were.

But this witch, never really thought about this, and she didn't even know how powerful they could be. She just knew, she had to eliminate them, no matter what. Now, all she had to think about was how to do it.

And she started the witchcraft work . . .

Chapter 3

I opened my eyes slowly.....

I opened my eyes slowly. My surroundings were still grey, but was starting to take shape,and I could see the scene before me much clearer. The trees were moving with the wind as if they were dancing. The birds and squirrels perched in the trees watching. Hazel was also lying down beside me, her fur shedding onto my jeans. I noticed that I wasn't in that part of the garden anymore. In fact, I might not have even been in a garden anymore. I spotted a long tower. It was made of oak and tree bark. Surrounding it were dozens of cherry blossom trees.

It was a beautiful sight.

There was a shadow of a girl in her teens with two large horns in the ear area. She was hard at work making and testing things with liquid. She suddenly turned her gaze towards me, then whispered: "You are her, and she's coming for you." As she pointed to me, then herself, then held out her bottles of questionable liquid.

Mist started to surround me. Her words rang in my head as I started crawling away from the tower. Three white figures came towards me. "She's coming for you, she's coming for you, she's coming for you." They whispered.

As I started to let out a raw scream, I woke up. Sweat was dripping down my forehead. *Just a bad dream.* I thought. There was still some mist around me.

I was back in my room. I got out of bed and yelled for my uncle. "HELLO?! UNCLE BRIAN WHERE ARE YOU?! Oh hey, Hazel, come with me." I started to panic. Then, I almost tripped. There, laying on the fluffy white carpet of my room, was the chain for the

lock that was on the door of the garden. That chain *never* comes *off* the door, unless something was seriously wrong.

Chapter 4

I frantically looked around.....

I frantically looked around the massive mansion for my uncle. Hazel just followed me around as I searched. What did the words that the girl said even mean? What if they had been warning me about something? What if I let another family member be in danger?

What if the girl who ruined my life is back?

No, that can't be. She's locked up forever.

I thought all these overwhelming thoughts as I quickly ran around the entire mansion, but Uncle Brian was nowhere in sight. I let out a deep breathe and slowly walked over to the door of the garden. *You're going to be alright; you're going*

to be fine; you will be JUST FINE, I told myself.

I started to sob violently again. I couldn't breath. I was shaking. I clung to my chest. No, this can't be happening right now. Not right now. Before it could get any worse, I stepped into the beam of light in the door. I felt a tug as I softly landed on the grass of the garden. There was a shy little girl with pigtails and small light denim overalls. She was holding a purple and pink teddy bear with a red heart in its chest.

I must have looked like I was a tomato drowning in tears because she looked at me with much sadness and concern. Her sad blue-grey eyes sparkled against the grey of the sky. I couldn't help but feel warm around her. She mentioned for me to follow her. She brought me to a part of the garden that had another oak door with a single rare lotus flower and vines. On the left was a pond with swans and ducks swimming around. She put her teddy bear on the ground and looked at me, eyes beaming. "I'm Maddie, and welcome to the garden, what's your name? How did you end up here?" The little girl said, first quietly, then more enthusiastically. "Hi,

I'm Maya, this is my dog, Hazel." I said just as Maddie pet Hazel softly. "So, um . . ." I continued. "The house next door is my uncle's and . . . ." I paused. Was it worth telling her about the past year? "Well, about a year ago, my family and I went on a road trip to Oregon, and then they were killed." I said. I had to leave out the part where I woke up screaming in the middle of the night. Every night. Or crying during the day. "Aw, I'm sorry, but seriously, you live THERE?" She asked, pointing to Uncle Brian's house. "That's the house everybody in this garden fears." Then she started to whisper: "Even Myera fears him and the power the house has."

"Who's Myera?" I asked. "Myera, is the feared child of Medusa (although she isn't very similar), she has been here for the past year and has been making trouble ever since! She has been destroying and enchanting everything and spends hours in the wooden tower in the heart of the garden. Nobody knows what she is working towards, but we know its going to be bad, and the crazy part is, around 6 months ago, the animals have disappeared and Myera has been working

harder and harder, and yet, no one knows why." Maddie spoke in a way so poetic I found myself captivated in listening to her words. As if they were a poem. Even Hazel seemed interested.

As all of this was being processed in my head, I realize that this is real. My dream could have been warning me about this Myera girl, witch, or whatever she was. And the tower too, it was shown in my weirdly clear and specific dream. "How do you know all this?" I asked Maddie when she stopped circling playfully around me.

She looked at me sadly. "My mom disappeared two years ago and I will never forget the day she told me her biggest secret. She had a garden in her childhood house where she grew up. When she took me there, she showed me the garden and a wooden door with a single rare flower that was only found in that area. She explained how the flower was the key to success, beauty, and enchantment. If found in the wrong hands, the flower could be used as a spell, and depending on how powerful the person is, could potentially end the world forever. Only a tiny percentage of the world, known as *idiosyncratic people*, have the power to stop it, but every time the flower was used to curse someone, that population was too late, or hadn't discovered their powers yet. And only about one tenth of that percentage found out their powers. She also let me into the oak door and we stepped in, but she disappeared into the light, and I never saw her again. Let me be honest with you, I am one of the people with the secret hidden powers.

My mom was also one of them. And I know she would want me to be helping anyone who stumbles upon our secret." Maddie said. I stared at her in amazement. "So, have you been here since you and your mom went through the door?" I asked her. "Yes." She answered sadly.

I wondered if she would ever find her again. Maybe at least she would get her mom back. "I know what you're thinking, and yes, my power is mind reading, but I've looked everywhere that I can, I haven't found her yet."

"Everywhere you can? Does that mean there are places you can't go?" I asked curiously.

Maddie sighed helplessly. "You have way too many questions girl." She said with a laugh. I grew anxious. I hate making people feel annoyed. "There is a part of the garden where Myera is, she has an oak tower where she works day and night, and she has protected it with some sort of thing, so if my mom, and maybe your uncle are there, we won't be able to get to them." She continued. "But the powers that people got were able to stop any witchcraft, so that means, if we round up and find most of the special people, and use the powers together, we could stop Myera!" I said.

I felt my brain finally working after such a long time. Maybe doing whatever this was would distract me from everything. An escape plan. One adventure to save myself. I started towards the oak door to get out of the garden so that we could start with this plan. But as I tried to pull the door open, the door wouldn't budge even an inch! "Uh, but slight problem." I said. "The door won't open."

Chapter 5

I was pacing back and forth,.....

I was pacing back and forth, trying to figure out what to do here. Maddie was looking up at the sky, whispering words I could not hear. Hazel just spun around, matching my energy.

"Wait, Maddie! Is there any way that you could tell what Myera is thinking right now? It could help us- somehow." I said quickly without thinking of what might happen. "Yes, I will, but first, I think I can somehow project it onto something so that we can both hear it." Maddie answered. She held her pointer finger to each side of her head. After about two minutes,

Maddie had created a clear image in the pond, and what it was showing was so bad, it could hurt so many people and nobody would even notice! Myera had a plan so evil, it was hard to imagine. The pond showed a girl with short, wavy brown hair with horns on her head mixing potions and liquids. She had glowing purple and red eyes as she stared at her evil potions. She looked oddly familiar. Her plan was to hypnotize the people and bring them to her, where she will then eliminate all their powers. The image in the pond showed Myera stabbing a teenage boy's wrist as he sat there, wailing, blood gushing out of him. He just lay there, dying.

We both gasped at the horrifying image. She took the powers out of his blood and stored it in a jar filled halfway with other people's pow-ers, just waiting to be made into something that could be very disastrous. I didn't dare think about what would happen if the jar completely filled up. As for the blood, to me and Maddie's surprise, Myera drank the blood straight from the cup she had poured it into, and as she swallowed the blood, her eyes stopped glowing and her whole face grew soft, her eyes turning to the colour of salt water. For a split second, she seemed to hesitate on her plans.

She looked like someone I never thought I would see again.

"Mom?" I cried just as she looked at me and the image in the pond cleared.

Before I knew it, I was kneeling on the perfectly green grass, feeling the tears running down my cheeks. Hazel rushed over to me and I cried into her fur. Maddie knelt beside me, rubbing my shoulder to comfort me. She said to me, "I have to tell you something. I lied to you in the beginning. My mom didn't disappear into the light she....my mother was caught doing witchcraft deep in this garden and was turned into an enchanted animal. She roamed the gardens for about two years before she was shot by ...It's hard to say this, but she was shot by your uncle. A little part of me said that she deserved it because witchcraft is the most appalling form of magic there is, but the rest of me cried and

cried, and I felt like I would never feel like my true being until finding out about my powers. That was when I felt good being able to always know what is on someone's mind. And as my mom always said, "As long as there is love and memory, there is no true loss." Maddie's words were so poetical I started calming down knowing there was someone that understood me even though our situations were different.

I stood up, clearing my throat; wiped my tears and quickly said, "I think we're running out of time, anybody else in the magical community could be next in Myera's evil plan, so I think we should recruit the 'magical' people in this area and round up as much of them as we can and try to save the hostages of Myera waiting to be killed by this elimination process, so we have to move quick." I finished. "But the oak door is somehow locked, so how do we get out?" Maddie questioned.

I went to the door and pulled (and pushed) as hard as I could and fell on my bum. I prayed greatly that I could actually do something. It has been so long since I actually got up on my butt and did anything at all. Don't get me wrong, I do my homework, but that only helps me get closer to getting a worthless piece of paper at the end of high school. Even if it creates the smallest dent, I want to take the credit, I want to know always and forever that I did something. Something amazing. Something that leaves a mark. Something good. And I want to always remember that it was me. Me, who did it. It is kind of selfish I know.

I put my head against the door and felt the design of the oak with my fingers and made lines as I closed my eyes. I concentrated and murmured, "Ever tried. Ever failed. No matter. Try again. Fail better." I smiled. "Did your mom ever say that to you?" Maddie said. I knew I couldn't say no because it was true, and she could literally read my mind. "Yeah, it truly gives me hope." I answered. I waited for her to say something else, but she was looking straight behind me. I turned around and to my surprise, there it was, the oak door swung open.

Chapter 6

"How did you do that?"

"How did you do that?" Maddie asked in awe. I shrugged. Me and Maddie slowly walked towards the oak door and stepped outside the garden for the first time since what felt like hours of talking and explaining. *What if, I was part of the population and I had... powers?* The thought sounded so ridiculous and childish.

Like something out of a book about *rainbows* and *fairies* and *magic*. But there was no other logical explanation to how I opened the door. "Could someone else be behind the door opening by itself?" Maddie said, reading my thoughts. I knew that she was reading my mind and searching deeper for how that happened. "Maya, you opened the door, and the only way to find out if you are part of the magical community is . . ." She paused. Then, out of nowhere a piece of shimmering purple cloth was wrapped around me. "What is happening?"

I asked. "This is the Cloth of Magic and if after the cloth is removed from your body, it starts flying, it means you are magical, and if its falls to the ground, you are just a normal being." Maddie answered me. After a minute, the cloth was removed, and to my surprise, it didn't fly nor fall. Instead, it floated and glowed a very light yellow. "Interesting." Maddie said.

"This reaction is very rare." "Well, what does it mean?" I asked, puzzled. "I'm not really sure, but it does signify that you are a magical being and you are more powerful than the rest of the normal population. But it also means you can control both witchcraft and magic itself. In most cases, the being can choose to be part of either the good or evil, since they're able to control both types. But again, it's very rare." Maddie spoke in a very scientific way, as if I

was a very interesting science project. I gasped at her knowledge and at this weird discovery about myself.

I sighed. I didn't want to be a special being. I didn't intend on actually being something special. I stared at my hands while they were trembling. Maddie rubbed my back in a way that made me feel warm.

Never, in my almost fourteen years of life, had I imagined this scene right here, and weirdly, I was grateful for it.

I made a good friend and a couple memories while it lasted.

And as much as everything hurts, she helped me open up empathetically in ways I could never have imagined.

Chapter 7

So, for the next hour or.....

So, for the next hour or so, I was either thinking of what to even start with, or, I was just sulking. Suddenly, I heard a faint and quiet whisper coming close. And closer . . . Then, out of the blue, came a ghostly girl. She seemed lonely and frightened. Though, as she got closer, I noticed that she was growing older, taller, even. Soon, she turned into a beautiful girl with luscious brown hair and bright blue eyes. She almost looked like . . . "MOM!" Maddie yelled.

Her mother started to reach out to her. They seemed to go into a hug. She even hugged me, but soon I realized that something was itching at me. Her hug was so familiar, the way she laughed, the way her hands felt smooth like

hand cream. As Maddie's mother morphed into my mother, I felt like I *needed* to breath, but I just couldn't. It felt as though my *soul* was getting stolen. It sounds stupid I know, but trust me, I *couldn't breath*. My fight or flight was getting tested. I guess I chose somewhat of a version of *fight*. I quickly snatched the flower on the oak door and shielded my face as if it was going to shield me from a gun. My mother stopped whatever she was doing quickly.

She stared hard at the flower, and just as suddenly as she came, she faded away into flower petals. Maddie seemed impressed, but the look on her face showed interest like there was something else she wasn't telling me. *Damn it! I wish I could read her mind like she can with mine.* I thought angrily. Suddenly a voice that sounded like Maddie ringed in my head.

"Why was she fighting her mom with her anger?"

"She was so smart to think of the rare flower trick."

"It's so weird how she's capable of both magic and witchcraft which is neither good nor bad."

"Her mother must have been capable of magic, but also witchcraft, explaining how she could have been Myera."

"But why? And I thought she died along with the rest of Maya's family. Gosh I feel so bad for her."

Why did she think all that? If I don't commit neither magic nor witchcraft, what does that make me? Am I an outcast again, even out of the *idiosyncratic* people? Am I just some *creature?* Anger boiled inside me. I started feeling like I *couldn't trust Maddie.* But I had to.

For now.

Slowly I felt this odd anger just jumping out. I felt a very strong light on my eyes. Then, everything became very black. Perhaps,the blackest of blacks, a flat black.

I was neither floating nor walking. I was just casually bouncing up and down the area. Out of nowhere, a creepy figure appeared. It was in the

shape of me and moved as I moved.

Just my own shadow.

Page: 37

I kept bouncing down what seemed to be a flat hallway that never seemed to end. I kept going anyways, until my shadow somehow stayed in front of me, not moving as I moved. It stopped me and I froze. The shadow started to grow tall. Then it started to shrink, and I watched in horror as the shadow turned out to be Myera. Her appearance was much different than how she looked before. She was much chubbier and had lots of warts on her misshaped face. Her hair was not brown anymore but an ugly black-green. *"Those are the effects of witchcraft."* I heard Maddie's poetic voice ring in my head.

She walked slowly towards me, and to my surprise, slapped me across the face, which unfortunately triggered a few terrifying memories.

I felt the burn on my cheek. Clutching my face, I looked around and in front of me was a middle-aged woman with brown hair, chubby cheeks, eyeliner, and bright red lipstick, along with layer after layer of shiny lip gloss. "MAYA

WILLOW ORTEGA! ARE YOU EVEN LISTENING TO ME?!"

It was the sound of my angry mother. I missed my mom a lot, but now, I remember all the memories of her saying I wasn't perfect, and how I was the worst daughter in the world when I got in trouble. But beyond that, I will always remember her sweet smile, her soft healing hands, her amusing laughter. "MAYA! Ugh, you never listen to me, you flawed young lady!" My mom stormed into another room. As soon as she left, my little sister walked into the room with a fearful look. She had been listening to the conversation the whole time. "Maya, is Mommy going to leave us? Like Daddy did?" Sabrina asked me with so much sadness in her eyes.

All was silent.

"No, of course not Sabrina." I said with so much pain in my voice.

Tears formed in my eyes as I thought about how much anger and sorrow I have stored in

my chest since I was 8 because of a stupid man who took his family for granted. I wiped the tears away and hugged Sabrina tightly.

Suddenly all the light seemed to disappear and now, everything was dark.

I was back in the dark hallway.

Sabrina started to grow older and taller too, then pulled me closer by the sleeve of my sweater. "How could you leave us outside the car when we were being freaking murdered!" My stomach cramped with guilt. "I was really upset that day from my fight with Evie, I didn't want to get out of the car, I didn't know that it was going to happen!" I said while blinking back tears.

"You are no sister of mine." Sabrina said coldly.

I am losing my love for you, her disdainful voice summarized. Before I could say anything else, a voice called, "SABRINA, COME HERE THIS INSTANT!" "Yes, mother." Was all that Sabrina replied and quickly dashed away. I looked in Sabrina's direction, then turned back to where I had been looking at. I saw myself looking straight into my older brother Toby's face. He looked depressed and sad, but serious. I quickly looked away before I made any eye contact with him. I looked down and saw Hazel lying beside Toby's legs.

Why is Hazel here? I thought as I bent down and scratched him behind the ears and pet his soft light brown fur. Tears started streaming down my face when I came to realization that my family was in heaven and I would actually never see them again.

As I was petting Hazel, Toby stood there, listening to the silence of the hallway. He suddenly made eye contact with me. "She wants to see you." He whispered. I looked at him confused. "Who?" I whispered back. "Who else? *Mother*." Toby replied coldly. We walked through the darkness until we finally reached an oak door. It looked strangely like the two oak doors in the garden. It also had the exact same rare flower held up by different coloured vines.

I wonder if Maddie is wondering where I am

or if I'm okay? Does she even care that much? I thought with a new, burning feeling in my chest. "Have fun." Toby said in a very off version of his funny sarcastic voice. I realized how much I miss him. He was never even close to being the best sibling, but we had good times. Good laughs.

Its time to move on, I told myself. After all, this is all a dream that will be gone in just a minute, with everyone included; I could finally get back to my plan.

The door suddenly swung open and there she was, inside the infamous oak tower, my mother. Keeping watch of everything outside it. I saw myself in the mirror.

I look just like her.

For a moment, I forgot everything about the fact that my mom was, or is Myera. That she is using magic (and witchcraft) for evil, or that she is in possession of a very rare flower. I just completely forgot. All I thought about was the murder of my mother and how much I missed and longed for her from the moment she lay bloody on the ground. All the flashbacks of the terrible evening that ruined my life. Her on the ground. Blood everywhere. Blood. Fear. Her worried expression, whatever it was, it never left her face. The face I so loved and always will. The now old face of my own mother who was always there for me. Tears rolled down my cheeks when I ran to hug her tightly. But just as I touched her, she and all my surroundings, the room, the dark hallway, disappeared and faded into the light.

Chapter 8

The light led me back .....

The light led me back to the garden where both Maddie and Hazel rushed over to me. "Okay, what the hell just happened?" Maddie asked, deeply concerned about me. Through my loud sobs I explained everything. From the flat dark hallway, to seeing Toby and Sabrina, and how I saw my mother. Maddie was really interested to know. After I was done, she said, "Well, while you were gone, I thought of something. Something big. So, you know how you thought about what would happen if

Myera completely filled up her jar of power?" I nodded. "Well, depending on what the power *really is*, I think that if the jar is full, there is literally nothing we can do. Myera is able to steal any magical being's heart and/or soul, using the potion." She stopped to get my reaction. I was listening but was also zoned out. Does she mean that, what happened with that ghost earlier . . . was a sign? Obviously, Maddie heard it and she suddenly went quiet. "I think, maybe you're right, it was a sign, a message. Just like those dreams you had, Maya. Myera has been calling you and giving you signs and clues since your family was . . . assassinated. She was calling you.

"She still is"

She was calling me all along? I slowly thought to myself. Why is this happening to me? All I want is to go to my bed and sleep for hours until the light of the next morning comes and I could wake up and see the face of Sabrina in our room. Our old room. "So, step 1, figure out how to recruit those people. Step 2, find my mom, and your uncle. Step 3, Find Myera, and step 4, save the idiosyncratic people from Myera." Maddie said only just thinking of the plan on the spot. "Step 4 seems like *a lot* of steps." I

said. "But let's go anyways." I continued.

Because we really are just winging it. And off we went. Out of the garden, out of the mansion, and onto the dark, empty streets.

An unlikely group. A thirteen-year-old, a nine-year-old and a golden retriever.

Chapter 9

We stood there for at least 15 minutes after we left the house. "How do we even start?" I said with impatience. "I guess we travel the world?" Maddie said with uncertainty. "No, there has to be a better way." I muttered to myself.

And then the whole world turned green. A dark, luscious green.

I opened my eyes to find tree branches in my face. Maddie and Hazel appeared behind me. We were all very confused. What had just happened? We were in what seemed to be another garden just like ours, but instead of an oak door, there was a door made of red cedar tree bark, but the flower on the door and everything

else was the same. I looked to my left and there it was, a giant house sitting right next to the garden. This made everything crystal clear to me. "No way!" Maddie said smiling. *Yes way!* I thought. I had brought us to one of the idiosyncratic people's homes with their own secret garden.

"Wait, so this means that the population that we call idiosyncratic, they all have a secret garden in their home? Does the person who built the houses know that the next owner is going to be one of them?" I ask. "No, I don't think so, I think that the secret garden is just a message, a sign that you are one of them, and it just moves in with you at every house." Maddie answered quickly. "Also, Maya, I mean obviously you are special like all of us, but even your power is special. You can both wish for something and even what you *think of* can come true . . . oh wait, let's hope that you haven't thought any bad things, but just, you know, be careful."

Be careful.

A phrase that has been said to me way too

many times throughout my life, and now, it just doesn't seem so possible anymore.

Chapter 10

We stayed there a while .....

We stayed there a while just staring at one of our fellow...idiosyncratic people's secret garden. They probably didn't even know that it was there. It took at least five minutes until I slowly walked towards their own garden's oak door. Maddie trailed behind. I opened the door, fearing what happened last time to happen again. When the light blinded me.

It did. But something unexpected happened.

I was floating somewhere, sort of downwards, with Hazel in my arms. It was as if I were falling, but very slowly. Maddie was there beside me this time.

There was a faint green glow below us, the part we were going towards. We suddenly landed with a thud. We were in another world of grass. Maddie stood up but as quickly as she did, she dropped to the ground again. I suddenly felt something tingly. My nose was filled with many exhausting scents, and I soon became weary and lay in the grass.

The last thing I remember seeing was a girl with blood smeared all over, standing above me, looking straight into my eyes, her icy blue eyes staring creepily right into my soul, before the whole world went black.

Again.

Chapter II

Something like this had .....

Something like this had happened to me before.

When I was 8 years old. It was the day after my father left. I shouldn't have cried the way I did that morning. Because he was never my *dad*, he was just my *father*.

But I cried. I cried so much I got dizzy and the world went dark. For hours. I would open my eyes now and then but the darkness was comforting. It distracted me from the pain.

I was in my bed for so long everyone was worried.

But no one was thinking about my mother.

Because she was the one who cared for him. All the years that they were married.

And he just left her like that.

After probably 3 whole days, I stirred out of bed.

I will never forget the anger on my mom's face.

I woke up, dizzy.

The world was blurry but it's starting to come into shape now.

Everywhere was misty.

My breathing was shaky.

The malodorous smell of the flowers exhausted me to an awful point.

Maddie woke up, half unconscious beside me.

I felt like I was trapped in a closet full of plants.

I tried to sit up but quickly fell back onto the grass, my eyes heavy, the world becoming dark again as I felt my heavy eyes close, fearing I may not open them again.

Chapter 12

The world was hazy .....

The world was hazy and misty.

I still lay unconscious on the grass. But I could make out some figures again.

A tall figure stood above me. "Don't forget.

Everyone will turn their back on you eventually. Even yourself. You are her Maya. <u>Her.</u> You know it. Don't even try to deny it."

I woke up feeling a sense of misunderstanding and heartbreak in my chest.

How long had I been unconscious? Is Maddie okay? Is she even here-?

Suddenly, everything went dark for maybe a fraction of a second, before a tall lady appeared before me. I stood up, ready to run. "Hey, its you!" She called out in a deep, alluring voice.

I was bewildered. It's me? What does that even mean? My eyebrows shot up to my hairline once I realized. "So, you are . . . me - from the future?" I asked. "Oh, don't sound so foolish and childish young lady, of course, yes, it is you that is me standing here.

You see, this whole situation, from the moment you family was murdered, sparked, how do I put this in words that you'll understand? Basically it formed a *crack* in the universe. Because, well, the universe was aware of the fact that something that reveals your whole entire future was put in your head. All the dreams and "visions" you've had the past, well exactly 368 days plus the days you've been in this whole new, strange world, were signs. You following? Okay great, I'm going to continue either way. And, here I am *continuing* to reveal your future because you would have either way found out when you would have come to stop me."

"Wait, you're Myera..." I reply. Suddenly, everything made sense. My mother's last words, my most recent vision. And I also realized that the Myera I saw in my visions were all me. Not my mother. *I am evil.* I turn out as an evil girl.

Something seemed to twist in me. Like it was being put into place. I realized that the always livid grey sky turned a deep blue. The wound in the universe was being restored. But the wound inside me is not. It never will be.

I realize what my future must be. I'm, as it turns out, a murderer. A killer.

Epilogue

So, there you have it, the most use-less survivor story ever told.

And yet, if you're reading this, that means that this was in some way intriguing for you. And that's great, really. I adore getting the recognition that I deserve, but, really think about it, what does liking the pain of this tale say about you, huh? Do you enjoy reading about the tragedies that go on in my head? That pain inside me, as agonizing as it is, I have to live with it. And I do live with it now.

This is just my life. At least, maybe I am still the greatest woman out there. At least, I did do something. Maybe, I finally am the best

at something. At least sooner rather than later, the wound in me will heal.

I'm glad to even be delusional about it because deep down I know that the wound inside me will never heal. It will always be there, burning and churning in my heart, haunting me with my past.

Sometimes the pain got so unbearable that I would daydream about my childhood. The days of running in fields, sunshine beaming on my face, path wide and open. I would just run and run, not knowing anything about the world, as I had not learned about the world yet, and the world had yet to hurt me.

Those memories were freedom as I knew it.

Until I would get to the memories of when my life went downhill.

That stupid, stupid day.

Sadly when I started to dream, I couldn't

stop. I remembered this dream vividly. I was hiding behind the car door, wind pushing at my face. It would start to rain soon, I would think, as I got up to grab my phone that was thrown across the pavement. I reached and reached, fingertips almost touching the edge of the screen, so close to grabbing and calling someone, anyone. And then I would hear the sharp ping of the knife slicing the air, dropping onto the ground. The ground in front of me. Inches away from my face.

I would slowly stand up, hoping the slower it took, the faster she would go away.

But she didn't. She stayed. In my head. And she would always stay. For the rest of my existence. I can't really call it life at this point, when I am only thinking of past memories, again and again.

I do realize that I am rambling again, but I can't help myself any more than I couldn't help them. Mom, Sabrina, and Toby. On that stupid, stupid day.

Had they been a dream? I ask myself with deep concern, because why couldn't I remember them?

Yet I could still hear her laugh. That deadly, horrifying laughter. Icy and cold, like the eyes that I couldn't stop looking at when we came face to face.

I don't know why I am like this. What the purpose is. Why it feels like an endless dream.

Endless yet painful. Oh, so painful. It burns.

And it won't stop. I don't know what I am supposed to do.

I don't know when I'm going to wake up again.

I woke up with a start, sweat dripping down my face, pooling into my tired eyes.

I felt confused because I was sure I'd had this dream before.

THE END

باغ جادو

و

جادوگر

نگارش: شایا معتمدی

مترجم: محمد آتش برگ

با الهام از «باغ اسرارآمیز»
نوشته فرانسیس هاجسون

سریال کتاب: P۲۵۱۵۲۵۰۲۷۰
عنوان: باغ جادو و جادوگر دو زبانه (فارسی - انگلیسی)
زیرنویس عنوان: با الهام از «باغ اسرارآمیز» نوشته فرانسیس هاجسون
نویسنده: شایا معتمدی
مترجم: محمد.ع آتش برگ
ویراستار: دکتر علی هاشمی
صفحه‌آرایی: مهری صفری
طراح جلد: محبوبه لعل‌پور
شابک/ ISBN: ۳-۲۷۶-۷۷۸۹۲-۱-۳۷۸
موضوع: داستان تخیلی نوجوانان، اسرارآمیز
مشخصات کتاب: قطع رقعی، جلد مقوایی
تعداد صفحات:۱۱۴   بخش فارسی:۵۰
تاریخ نشر ادیشن فارسی:می ۲۰۲۶
انتشارات در کانادا: انتشارات بین‌المللی کیدزوکادو

KIDSOCADO PUBLISHING HOUSE
VANCOUVER, CANADA

تلفن: ۷۲۴۸ ۳۳۳ (۲۳۶) ۱+
واتس آپ: ۷۲۴۸ ۳۳۳ (۲۳۶) ۱+
ایمیل: info@kidsocado.com
وب‌سایت: https://www.kidsocado.com

تقدیم به مادرم

این نخستین کتاب من است

نخستین بار که چیزی را به دیگران، از صمیم دل تقدیم می‌کنم! پس،

البته باید هم تقدیم به شما مادر عزیزم باشد.

خوشحالی من حد و مرز ندارد،

چون که شما مرا تشویق کردید که کتاب را بنویسم.

بی نهایت شما را دوست دارم.

شایا

"تمام اسبان و همه‌ی مردان پادشاه نتوانستند،

دوباره مرا سرِ هم کنند."

تیلور سوئیفت

پیشگفتار

می‌دانی که مردم همیشه یک حرف را می‌گویند: «این روزهایِ سخت است که تو را نیرومندتر می‌سازد.»

خب، فکر می‌کنم هر چه باشد، آنچه اینجا می‌نویسم، دقیقاً همان معنا را در خود دارد.

نه، آن دروغ است.

می‌بینی چقدر آسان است وانمود کنیم که خوشحال و قوی هستیم؟ می‌دانم مردم نیز می‌گویند: «تظاهر کن تا زمانی که واقع بشود.»

اما من آن‌قدر طولانی‌مدت تظاهر کرده‌ام که انگار یادم رفته چطور احساسات واقعی و خالص خودم را نشان بدهم.

پس می‌بینی، حالم خوب نیست، بنابراین حتی اگر در این قصه کمی هم احمق به نظر بیایم، لطفاً بر من سخت نگیر.

حالا که مقدمه کنار رفته، بگذار بگویم که این داستان برای آدم‌هایی مثل تو است که از درون زخمی‌اند.

افرادی که وانمود می‌کنند حالشان خوب است، اما خشمی درون آن‌ها است که منتظر بیرون زدن است. در جمع دیگران لبخند می‌زنند، اما وقتی به خانه می‌آیند، به داخل حمامشان که صدا از آن بیرون نمی‌آید می‌روند، آنوقت به نوعی گریه و زاری می‌کنند که انگار بار اول است این حال را تجربه می‌کنند در حالی که هر روز انجام می‌دهند.

این داستان قرار نیست پیامی بدهد و بگوید:

«همه چیز درست می‌شود.»

چونکه اینطوری نیست.

خب، در مورد من اینطوری نبود.

خواهی دید.

فصل ۱

هوا سرد بود. . . . . .

هوا سرد بود. من خودم را پشت خودروی شاسی بلند[1] سفید، به حالت خمیده، قایم کرده بودم و یواشکی بالا را نگاه می‌کردم، مامانم، خواهر کوچکم، سابرینا[2] و بردار بزرگم توبی[3]، کنار جاده دراز به دراز افتاده بودند، و خون همه جا جاری شده بود. خیلی دلم می‌خواست می‌توانستم با تمام توان به سوی آنان بدوم و آنقدر گریه کنم که دیگر اشکی از چشمم بیرون نیاید. اما او هنوز آنجا بود. چاقو در دست، با پوزخندی بر صورت رنگ پریده گچ مانندش، آهسته گام بر می‌داشت. همه چیز در سکوت فرو رفته بود.

تا اینکه صدای مادرم را شنیدم.

«مایا[4]، تو باید خیلی مواظب باشی. تو هم اویی. او .... تو هستی...»

مادر وقت نداشت جمله‌اش را تمام کند و هیچگاه هم نخواهد داشت.

روی شکم خود، پشت خودرو دراز کشیدم، روده‌ام پیچ خورده و با هر نفس درد در دلم می‌پیچید. می‌لرزیدم، قلبم تند می‌تپید، داشت از سینه‌ام، بیرون

1- SUV
2- Sabrina
3 -Toby
4 -Maya

می‌زد، درد به قفسه سینه و دنده‌ام می‌زد. می‌خواستم همان‌جا دراز بکشم و گریه کنم؛ در عوض احساس ترس و تقصیر کردم سعی کردم تلفنم را بردارم. از گوشه چشم سایه‌ای را دیدم. صدای افتادن چاقو در هوا پیچید خیلی زود، من با چهره‌ی ترسناکش رو در رو شدم. چشمان آبی و یخ‌زده‌اش در تاریکی برق می‌زد. خنده‌ای کرد.

با وحشت از خواب پریدم. عرق از صورتم می‌چکید. در یک سال گذشته، دقیقاً همین خواب را بارها دیده‌ام و ظاهراً نمی‌توانم از آن بگذرم. بدنم از کمبود خوابی آرام، درد می‌کرد.

«این زندگی تو است. سال‌های گذشته همین بوده، پس بلند شو و سعی کن و از آن رد شو، همانطور که همیشه این کار را انجام می‌دهی.»

من با اعتماد به نفس این حرف را به خودم زدم.

با شتاب برای صرف صبحانه از پله‌های بلند و مرمری پایین رفتم و باین ترتیب از همه اتاق‌های خالی عبور می‌کردم. از کنار تنها اتاق خانه که در بسته بود، گذشتم. با سه قفل اتاق را قفل کرده بودند. دوتا از قفل‌ها باز شده بودند و کلیدها روی فرش سبز جلوی در اتاق افتاده بودند. لحظه‌ای وسوسه شدم، اما چاره‌ای نداشتم، باید سریع برای صرف صبحانه به پایین می‌رفتم. عمو برایان، مشغول درست کردن تُست فرانسوی و تخم‌مرغ هم‌زده بود. از مهربانی‌اش دلم آشوب شد. هیچگاه با وی حرف نمی‌زدم. و بابتش احساس بدی دارم. او هرگز کار بدی در حقم نکرده اما نمی‌دانم چرا هیچ احساسی ندارم که بتوام گفت و گویی کاملاً عادی و معمولی با او داشته باشم.

سریع صبحانه خوردم و برای رفتن به مدرسه حاضر شدم. پس از این همه اتفاقی که افتاده بود، من قاعدتاً نباید به مدرسه می‌رفتم. منصفانه نیست که مجبور شوم هر روز خودم را در دست‌شویی دختران حبس کنم تا بتوانم اشک بریزم. فکر کردن به آن....، به همه‌ی آن‌ها....، قلبم را می‌سوزاند.

به چهره‌های دردکشیده‌شان، درست پیش از آن‌که قلب‌هایشان از کار بیفتد. به لحظه‌ای که مادرم می‌خواست دستش را دراز کند و گونه‌ام را لمس کند، و من همان‌جا کنارشان نشسته بودم، با سر فرو رفته در دستان خون‌آلودم گریه می‌کردم.

هیچ‌کس نمی‌تواند بداند در چنین حالتی از اندوه، چه احساسی دارد. و البته من هم قرار نیست برایشان بگویم.

من، کمی پیش از اینکه بروم، هیزل[1] سگم را بغل کردم. نفسی عمیق کشیدم و در همان حال از در بیرون رفتم. روزی آفتابی بود.

چمن‌ها سبز و آسمان آبی بود؛ بچه‌ها می‌خندیدند و در خیابان می‌دویدند، اما من جرأت نداشتم به آنان نگاه کنم. چون خاطرات را یادآوری می‌کرد، خاطره‌های شیرین زندگی گذشته و همین دردناک‌ترشان می‌کرد. پس، من افکارم را به عقب ذهن فرستادم تا اینکه در عقب‌ترین گوشه ذهنم جای گرفت.

تمام روز را مثل همیشه گذراندم، چون من می‌بایست از برخورد با ایوی[2] بهترین دوست قدیمی خودم، خودداری می‌کردم. چون اگر دعوایی که او شروع کرده بود پیش نمی‌آمد و من هم با خانواده‌ام بیرون می‌رفتم.

گاهی دوست دارم فکر کنم به نوعی مرگ را فریب داده‌ام؛ به خاطر همان دعوا. اما این فکر کمکی نمی‌کند به این واقعیت که حالا کاملاً

1- Hazel
2- Evie

تنها هستم.به جز "هیزل"، سگم، که خیلی خوشحالم که از آن حادثه جان سالم بدر برد و با من است. از همه فاصله گرفتم. در هر حال، انگار برای هیچ‌کس مهم نیست که با من حرف بزند یا نه. بعضی‌ها وانمود می‌کنند برایم ناراحتند، اما در واقع با لحنی تمسخرآمیز دلسوزی می‌کنند؛ بعضی دیگر بی‌تفاوت‌اند، و بعضی هم فکر می‌کنند همه چیز را من ساخته‌ام. آخر مگر چند نفر هستند که تمام خانواده‌شان در یک سفر جاده‌ای با چاقو کشته شده باشند؟

وقتی به خانه رسیدم، برای خودم ساندویچ محبوبم را درست کردم، ساندویچ NPB یعنی نوتلا/کره بادام زمینی و موز، و بسوی دری رفتم که امروز صبح دیده بودم. کلید را برداشتم و قفل در را باز کردم. تابش نور سفید شدید جلوی چشمم بود. وارد اتاق شدم، گذاشتم کنجکاوی بر من غلبه کند. هیزل هم با من آمد. او ماده سگ ماجراجوی خوشگلی است.

اتاق، واقعاً "اتاق" نبود؛ بیشتر شبیه یک باغ بود. یک باغ اسرارآمیز. با خودم گفتم، شبیه آن کتاب است. با این‌حال، هرگز چنین باغی را جلوی خانه ندیده بودم، با اینکه از پنجره می‌شد تا آخر جاده را دید. از چیزی که یافته بودم، شگفت‌زده بودم و لبخند کوچکی ناخواسته روی لبم نشست. چمن‌ها سبزترین چیزی بودند که تا به‌حال دیده بودم، و گل‌ها در رنگ‌های گوناگون می‌درخشیدند. وقتی از زمین به بالا نگاه کردم، دوباره، می‌توانستم برق سفید درخشان را در آسمان ببینم و لحظه‌ای بعد، همه چیزهای اطراف من، حتی لباس‌های من، به‌رنگ خاکستری مات در می‌آمد. من گرمکن عنابی مورد علاقه‌ام را با شلوارجین گشاد سورمه‌ای پوشیده بودم. موهای خرمائی کوتاه من از روی صورتم ریخته بود و آنها هم خاکستری شده بود. حتی هیزل هم خاکستری بود. راستش را بخواهید دیدن او در آن وضعیت تیره بی روح، غم‌انگیز بود.

از گوشه‌ی چشمم دری دیدم که برگ‌های درخت مو روی آن را پوشانده بود، من هنوز خاکستری بودم. اما عجیب این بود که درب، تنها چیز رنگارنگ در تمام باغ بود. بسوی در رفتم و آن را با احتیاط و دقت بیشتر نگاه کردم. تکْ گُلی دیدم که در تمام باغ نظیرش را ندیدم. یک گل نیلوفر به رنگ آبی، با رگه‌هایی ظریف از سبز و آبی درخشان.

به محض این که با کنجکاوی در چوبی را باز کردم، نور زرد رنگ شدیدی باغ را فراگرفت و من با حالت تهوع بر زمین افتادم. آخرین چیزی که بخاطر می‌آورم این بود که دخترکی چندش‌آور و ترسناک سراپا خون بالای سرم ایستاده بود، مرا نگاه می‌کرد. چشمانم را بستم تا او را نبینم....

اما نتوانستم جلوی فریادم را بگیرم.

«آهای مایا، بریم هوا بخوریم!» صدای مادرم بود که با هیجان مرا صدا می‌کرد. به آرامی چشمانم را باز کردم. و به اطرافم نگاه کردم، به محیطی تازه که به طرز عجیبی در آن، صدای دل‌انگیز مادرم را می‌شنیدم. انگار هرگز آن حادثه رخ نداده بود. انگار خانواده‌ام در جلو چشمانم به نحوی وحشیانه کشته نشده بودند.

«خدای من، مایا، از اتاقت بزن بیرون، ما داریم می‌ریم کمی قدم بزنیم، زودباش!»

صدای برادرم بود که این حرف‌ها را با همان لحن مسخره گذشته به‌من می‌زد. حتی ژست قشنگِ قدیمی خود را هم نشان داد، مچ دستش را پائین آورد و قفل کرد. ما خندیدیم. از خنده روده‌بُر شدیم. حس کردم خنده الان عجیب باشد. احساس کردم درست مثل این است که دارم خواب می‌بینم

از زمانِ قتل تا این لحظه، هیچ‌وقت دوباره احساس خوشحالی نکرده بودم. اما من با آنچه داشت بر سرم می‌آمد، همراه می‌شدم و از اتاقم در آمدم و برای قدم زدن بیرون زدم. هوا هنوز بوی نمک می‌داد و آسمان و تمامی پیرامون من، همانند باغ، خاکستری بود.

ناگهان به سرفه افتادم، اما هیچ‌کس به کمکم نیامد. در همان لحظه، واقعیتِ مرگشان ناگهان بر من فرود آمد. آن‌ها واقعاً رفته بودند... و من واقعاً، کاملاً، تنها بودم. هیزل، کنار من نشست و آنچه می‌توانستم بشنوم، سکوت حیاطِ جلوی من بود.

فصل ۲

برای متروکه‌ها، روز عادی بود. . . . .

روزِ عادی‌ای بود برای برج متروکه‌ای که مرگبارترین موجودات در آن زندگی می‌کردند، و تقریباً روزی معمولی برای خانه‌ی وحشتناکی که در کنار آن برج قرار داشت. خانه‌ای که انسان‌ها در آن زندگی می‌کردند. از وقتی دختری زیبا با چشمان درخشان و لباسی بلند وارد آن‌جا شده بود، موجوداتِ درون برج پنهان شده بودند، و باغ بزرگ اطراف برج حالا وهم‌انگیز و در سکوتی مرگبار فرو رفته بود.

اما در خودِ برج، اوضاع متفاوت بود؛ آنجا پر از آشوب، دود و بی‌نظمی بود. او همان‌جا نشسته بود، کنار دیگِ جهنمیِ افسانه‌ای، جایی که بسیاری از موجودات جاد و شده، نابود شده یا به قتل رسیده بودند. در ذهنش نقشه‌ای شوم و رازآلود جریان داشت نقشه‌ای برای از میان بردن انسان‌های خاص در این دنیا.

او دختری خطرناک و اسرارآمیز بود: مایرا[1]، نامش از واژه‌ی مایرز (Myers) گرفته شده بود، به معنی «شیطان».

1- Myera

پلیس بارها تلاش کرده دختر را ردیابی کند و او را بگیرد، اما غیر ممکن بود؛ چون او حالا تقریباً توقف‌ناپذیر شده بود. تنها کسی که می‌توانست او را متوقف کند، هنوز از قدرت واقعی خود هیچ آگاهی نداشت. اما این مایرای جادوگر هرگز به آن فکر نکرده بود و نمی‌دانست که آن شخص تا چه اندازه نیرومند است.

دختر فقط می‌دانست که باید آنان را معدوم کند. چگونه، اصلاً مهم نیست. اکنون مجبور بود فکر کند **چطور باید این کار را انجام دهد.**

و سپس، کارِ جادوگری آغاز شد.....

فصل ۳

آرام، چشمانم را باز کردم. . . . .

آرام، چشمانم را باز کردم. همه چیز هنوز خاکستری بود، اما کم‌کم شروع به شکل‌گیری می‌کرد و من می‌توانستم صحنه روبروی خودم را روشن‌تر ببینم. درختان با باد حرکت می‌کرد، انگار می‌رقصیدند. پرندگان و سنجاب‌ها بر شاخه‌های درختان، نشسته و تماشایم می‌کردند. هیزل نیز، کنارِ من دراز کشیده بود. و موهایش روی شلوار جینِ من ریخته بود. متوجه شدم دیگر در آن قسمت باغ نیستم. در واقع انگار در هیچ باغی نیستم. برجی بلند را دیدم، ساخته شده از چوب بلوط و پوست درخت. دور تا دورش را ده‌ها درخت شکوفه گیلاس احاطه کرده بودند. منظره خیره‌کننده‌ای بود.

در سایه، دختری نوجوان را دیدم با دو شاخ بزرگ در ناحیه‌ی گوش‌ها. سخت مشغول ساختن و آزمایش مایعاتی ناشناخته بود.

ناگهان نگاهش را به من دوخت و در حالی که به من اشاره می‌کرد، زیر لب زمزمه کرد: «تو اویی... و او دارد سراغت می‌آید.»

به من اشاره کرد، بعد به خودش، و سپس شیشه‌هایی از مایعی مشکوک را بالا گرفت.

مهی غلیظ شروع کرد به پیچیدن دورم. کلماتش در ذهنم می‌پیچیدند، درحالی که به سختی از برج دور می‌شدم.

سه پیکره‌ی سفید از میان مه به سویم آمدند. با صدایی زمزمه‌وار تکرار کردند: «او دارد سراغت می‌آید... او دارد سراغت می‌آید... او دارد سراغت می‌آید...»

درست همان وقتی که شروع به جیغ زدن کردم، از خواب پریدم. قطره‌های عرق، از پیشانی‌ام، می‌چکید. با خودم گفتم:

«فقط یک کابوس و خواب آشفته بود.»

اما هنوز کمی مه دور و برم بود.

دوباره در اتاق خودم بودم. از تختم پائین پریدم و با فریاد عمویم را صدا زدم.

«آهای عموبرایان کجا هستید، کجا هستید؟!» بعد گفتم: «هی، هیزل، با من بیا» ، احساس وحشت تمام وجودم را گرفت.

بعدش، تقریباً داشتم می‌افتادم. روی فرش سفید و نرم اتاقم زنجیری افتاده بود؛ همان زنجیرِ قفلی که روی درِ باغ بود. و آن زنجیر هرگز از در جدا نمی‌شد... مگر اینکه اتفاقی واقعاً جدی افتاده باشد.

فصل ۶

با ترس و وحشت به اطراف خانه بزرگ عمویم نگاه کردم. همان‌طور که جست‌وجو می‌کردم، هیزل هم دنبالم می‌آمد. با خودم می‌گفتم حرف‌های آن دختر واقعاً چه معنائی می‌توانست داشته باشد؟ خوب، اگر درباره چیزی، به من هشدار می‌دهد، آنوقت چی؟ اگر باز بگذارم، یکی دیگر از اعضای خانواده‌ام، به خطر، بیفتد، چه می‌شود؟

اگر آن دختر ترسناکی که زندگی مرا ویران کرد، برگشته باشد چه؟

نه امکان ندارد. او برای همیشه در آنجا زندانی شده است.

با همین افکار آشفته در سراسر عمارت دویدم، اما هیچ نشانی از عمو برایان نبود. نفسی عمیق کشیدم و آرام به سمت درِ باغ رفتم. با خودم تکرار کردم: «همه‌چیز درست می‌شود... حالت خوب می‌شود... تو کاملاً خوب خواهی بود...»

اما ناگهان دوباره بی‌اختیار زار زدم. نفسم بند آمده بود، بدنم می‌لرزید. دست‌هایم را روی سینه‌ام فشردم. نه... نه، الان نه، نباید دوباره اتفاق بیفتد. پیش از آنکه اوضاع بدتر شود، قدم در پرتوی نور درِ باغ گذاشتم. احساسی

شبیه کشیده شدن به من دست داد و ناگهان نرم روی چمن‌های باغ فرود آمدم. دختربچه‌ای خجالتی با موی دُماسبی شده و لباس سرهمی جین روشن مقابلم بود.

در آغوشش عروسک خرسی (تدی بئر[1] ) بنفش و صورتی کوچکی نگه داشته بود که قلبی قرمز در سینه‌اش داشت. من احتمالاً بخاطر گریه‌هایی که کرده بودم می‌بایست شبیه گوجه فرنگی سرخ به نظر برسم، چون او با نگاهی پر از غم و دلسوزی نگاهم کرد. چشمان آبی-خاکستری غمگینش در تضاد با آسمان خاکستری برق می‌زد، و من بی‌اختیار احساس گرم درونم حس کردم.

با اشاره از من خواست دنبالش بروم. مرا به بخشی از باغ برد که در آن دری از چوب بلوط قرار داشت. پوشیده از پیچک‌ها و تنها یک تک گل نیلوفر آبی کمیاب روی آن بود. حوضچه‌ای در قسمت چپ قرار داشت که قوها و مرغابی‌ها در آن شنا می‌کردند. دخترک عروسک خرسی خود را روی زمین گذاشت و بمن نگاه کرد. چشمانش از خوشحالی برق می‌زد.

«من مَددی[2] هستم. به باغ خوش آمدی، چطوری به اینجا رسیدی؟» دخترک کوچک این حرف‌ها را اول به آرامی و سپس با هیجان بیشتر گفت. در همان حال که مَددی به نرمی هیزل را نوازش می‌کرد، گفتم:

«سلام، من مایا هستم. این هم هیزل سگ من است.» ادامه دادم:

«خب... خونه‌ی بغلی مال عمومه و...» مکث کردم. آیا ارزشش را داشت همه چیز را برایش تعریف کنم؟ بالاخره گفتم:

---

1 -Teddy Bear

2 - Maddie

«حدود یک سال پیش من و خانواده‌ام به سفر جاده‌ای به اورِگان رفتیم... و بعد... اون‌ها کشته شدند.»

نمی‌توانستم بگویم که از آن زمان هر شب با فریاد از خواب می‌پرم یا روزها با اشک بیدار می‌شوم. دخترک گفت:

«وای، متأسفم، اما براستی، تو آنجا زندگی می‌کردی؟» و با انگشت به خانه عمو برایان اشاره می‌کرد.

«آن خانه‌ای است همه‌ی آدم‌های این باغ از آن می‌ترسند.»

بعدش، پچ پچ کنان گفت: «حتی مایرا هم از او و قدرت آن خانه می‌ترسد.» پرسیدم:

«مایرا کیه؟» گفت:

«مایرا دختر ترسناک مدوسا است، (هرچند خیلی شبیه او نیست) تمام سال گذشته را اینجا بوده و تمام مدت دردِسر درست می‌کرده! همه‌چیز را ویران و نابود می‌کرد و ساعت‌ها در برج چوبین واقع در وسط و قلب باغ می‌نشست. هیچکس نمی‌دانست مشغول چه کاری است. ولی ما می‌دانستیم که نتیجه بد خواهد بود. قسمت وحشتناک‌تر قضیه این بود که حدود شش ماه پیش گم شدن حیوانات شروع شد و مایرا سخت‌تر و سخت‌تر کار می‌کرد و هنوز کسی نمی‌دانست که چرا؟»

مدّی طوری شاعرانه حرف می‌زد که محو صدایش شدم؛ انگار شعر می‌خواند. حتی هیزل هم با دقت گوش می‌داد. همه این موارد در سرم می‌گذشت، فهمیدم که همه چیز واقعی است. خواب می‌توانست هشداری به من در مورد مایرا این دختر جادوگر یا هرچه بود، باشد. برج هم در خواب مسخره من روشن و واضح دیده می‌شد. وقتی مدّی، بازی چرخیدن

دور من را متوقف کرد، ازش پرسیدم: «چطوری همه‌ی این‌ها را می‌دونی؟»
با نگاه غمناک به من نگریست و گفت:

«مادرم دو سال پیش ناپدید شد، و هرگز روزی را که بزرگترین راز را به من گفت، فراموش نمی‌کنم. مادرم، باغی در خانه کودکیش که در آن بزرگ می‌شد داشت و هنگامی که، مرا به آن خانه برد، باغ و در چوبی همراه با تک گل کمیاب را نشان داد که فقط در آن نواحی وجود داشت. مادرم توضیح داد، چطوری آن گل، کلید موفقیت، زیبایی و شعف بود. اگر این گل در دست‌های نادرست باشد، می‌تواند به عنوان جادو مورد استفاده قرار گیرد و چنانچه صاحب آن دست نیرومندی باشد، بالقوه می‌تواند برای همیشه به حیات گیتی، پایان بخشد. فقط درصد خیلی کوچکی از مردم، که بهشون می‌گن افراد خاص، قدرت متوقف کردن اون طلسم رو دارن. ولی هر بار که از گل برای طلسم استفاده شده، اون آدم‌ها یا دیر رسیدن، یا هنوز از قدرتشون خبر نداشتن. و فقط حدود یک‌دهم از اون‌ها، موفق شدن توانایی خودشون رو کشف کنن. بعد مادرم درِ بلوطی رو باز کرد و با هم داخل شدیم... اما او درون نور ناپدید شد و دیگه هیچ‌وقت ندیدمش. راستش رو بخوای، من یکی از اون آدم‌هایی‌ام که قدرت‌های پنهان دارن، و مادرم هم یکی از اون‌ها بود. می‌دونم اگه اینجا بود، از من می‌خواست به هرکسی که به این راز برخورد، کمک کنم.»

با حیرت به او نگاه کردم. پرسیدم:

«یعنی از وقتی با مادرت وارد اون در شدی، اینجا موندی؟» او با اندوه گفت: «بله.»

با خودم فکر کردم آیا هرگز دوباره مادرش را پیدا می‌کند؟ شاید بتواند دوباره او را در آغوش بگیرد.

مدّی لبخند تلخی زد و گفت: «می‌دونم داری به چی فکر می‌کنی، و بله، قدرت من ذهن‌خوانیه. اما هر جا که تونستم گشتم، هنوز پیداش نکردم.»

پرسیدم: «هر جا که تونستی؟ یعنی جاهایی هم هست که نمی‌تونی بری؟»

مدّی با ناامیدی آهی کشید: «وای، تو خیلی سؤال می‌پرسی، دختر!»

و خندید. دلواپس شدم؛ از اینکه شاید ناراحتش کرده باشم. او ادامه داد: «یه بخش از باغ هست که مایرا اونجاست. اون برج چوبی خودش رو داره که شب و روز توش کار می‌کنه، و با چیزی جادوش کرده، پس اگه مادرم، و شاید عموی تو، اونجا باشن، ما نمی‌تونیم بهش دسترسی پیدا کنیم.»

گفتم: «اما قدرتی که این آدم‌های خاص دارن، می‌تونه هر جادویی رو متوقف کنه، درسته؟ پس اگه بتونیم بیشترشون رو پیدا کنیم و با هم کار کنیم، می‌تونیم مایرا رو متوقف کنیم!»

احساس کردم مغزم بعد از مدت‌ها دوباره کار می‌کند. شاید این کار بتواند ذهنم را از همه‌ی دردها دور کند، یک نقشه برای فرار.

ماجرایی برای نجات خودم.

به سمت درِ بلوطی رفتم تا از باغ بیرون برویم و شروع کنیم، اما هر چه در را کشیدم، حتی یک ذره هم تکان نخورد!

گفتم: «اوه، فقط یه مشکل کوچیک...»

مدّی پرسید: «چی شده؟»

و من نفس‌زنان گفتم:

«در باز نمی‌شه!»

فصل ۵

جلو و عقب گام بر می‌داشتم . . . . . .

بی‌قرار، این سو و آن سو می‌رفتم. سعی می‌کردم بفهمم باید چه بکنم. مدّی به آسمانِ بالای سرش نگاه می‌کرد و کلماتی را به آهستگی زیر لب نجوا می‌کرد که نمی‌توانستم بفهمم چه می‌گوید. هیزل هم دور من می‌چرخید و مرا تقلید می‌کرد. با عجله گفتم: «صبر کن مدّی! آیا می‌تونی بفهمی مایرا الان داره به چی فکر می‌کنه؟ شاید این‌طوری بتونیم یه راه پیدا کنیم.»

مدّی جواب داد: «آره، می‌تونم... اما فکر می‌کنم بتونم افکارش رو به شکلی بیرونی هم نشون بدم تا هر دومون ببینیم.»

انگشت اشاره‌اش را دو طرف شقیقه‌هایش گذاشت. بعد از حدود دو دقیقه، تصویری شفاف در سطح برکه شکل گرفت و آنچه نشان می‌داد خیلی وحشتناک بود و می‌توانست به بسیاری از مردم آسیب برساند، و هیچکس هم حتی متوجهش هم نشود!

مایرا یک نقشه خیلی شیطانی داشت که حتی تصورش هم سخت بود. برکه، دختری را نشان می‌داد با موهای قهوه‌ای کوتاه و موج‌دار، و دو شاخ روی سرش، در حالی‌که مایع‌ها و معجون‌هایی را با دقت مخلوط می‌کرد. وقتی به

معجون‌های شیطانی خود خیره شده بود، چشمانش قرمز و مایل به ارغوانی براق بود. چهره‌اش عجیب آشنا به نظر می‌رسید. برنامه‌اش این بود که مردم را هیپنوتیز کند و به نزد خود آورد و سپس تمام نیروهای جادویی‌شان را از آن‌ها بگیرد.

تصویر در برکه نشان می‌داد که مایرا مچ دست پسر نوجوانی را با خنجر می‌درد، در حالی‌که او با فریاد از درد بر خود می‌پیچد و خون از او جاری است. او همان‌جا افتاد... در حال مرگ.

هر دوی ما از وحشت نفس‌مان بند آمد. مایرا قدرت آن پسر را از خونش بیرون کشید و در شیشه‌ای ریخت که نیمه‌اش از نیروی دیگران پر بود، شیشه‌ای که به نظر می‌رسید آماده‌ی ساخت چیزی فاجعه‌بار است. جرئت فکر کردن به این‌که اگر شیشه پر شود چه می‌شود را نداشتم.

اما ناگهان، کاری کرد که من و مدّی را شوکه کرد مایرا خون را از همان فنجانی که در آن ریخته بود، نوشید. وقتی آن را بلعید، چشمانش از درخشش افتادند، چهره‌اش نرم و آرام شد، و رنگ چشمانش به آبیِ آبِ شور تغییر کرد. برای لحظه‌ای کوتاه، گویی در تصمیمش مردد ماند. او شبیه کسی بود که هرگز تصور نمی‌کردم دوباره ببینمش.

«مامان؟»

با صدایی لرزان فریاد زدم درست همان لحظه که او به من نگاه کرد و تصویر از میان رفت. پیش از آنکه بفهمم چه شده، روی چمن‌های سبز زانو زده بودم، و اشک‌ها روی گونه‌هایم جاری بودند. هیزل خودش را به من رساند و من صورتم را در میان موهایش پنهان کردم و گریستم. مدّی کنارم نشست و دستش را روی شانه‌ام گذاشت تا آرامم کند. آهسته گفت:

«باید یه چیزی رو بهت بگم. من دروغ گفتم...»

«مامانم توی نور ناپدید نشد. او در اعماق همین باغ، حین انجام جادوگری دستگیر شد و به شکل حیوانی افسون‌شده درآمد. حدود دو سال در باغ پرسه می‌زد، تا این که... شلیک شد. سختِ گفتنش، اما کسی که به او شلیک کرد، عموی تو بود..»

اشک در چشمانش جمع شد.

«یه بخشی از وجودم می‌گفت که حقش بود، چون جادوگری خطرناک‌ترین نوع سحر در جهانه، اما بقیه‌ی وجودم فقط گریه می‌کرد. احساس می‌کردم تا وقتی قدرت‌هام رو نشناسم، خودِ واقعیم نیستم. وقتی فهمیدم می‌تونم ذهن دیگران رو بخونم، حس خوبی داشتم، چون بالاخره تونستم بدون ترس بدونم مردم واقعاً به چی فکر می‌کنن. و همون‌طور که مادرم همیشه می‌گفت: تا زمانی که عشق و یاد وجود داره، هیچ از دست‌دادی واقعی نیست..»

حرف‌های شاعرانه‌اش آرامم کرد. حس کردم بالاخره کسی هست که من را می‌فهمد، حتی اگر دردهایمان فرق داشته باشد. بلند شدم، نفسی عمیق کشیدم، اشک‌هایم را پاک کردم و با صدایی محکم گفتم:

«فکر می‌کنم زمان داره تموم می‌شه. هرکسی از دنیای جادویی ممکنه قربانی نقشه‌ی شیطانی مایرا بشه. باید آدم‌های جادویی این منطقه رو جمع کنیم و تا می‌تونیم ازشون کمک بگیریم. باید گروگان‌هایی رو که منتظر مرگ به‌دست مایرا هستن نجات بدیم. باید سریع عمل کنیم!»

مدّی گفت:

«اما درب چوب بلوطی، به نحوی قفل شده، پس چطور قراره بیرون بریم؟»

رفتم سراغ در و با تمام توان کشیدم (و فشار دادم) اما تعادلم را از دست دادم و روی زمین افتادم. با تمام وجود دعا کردم که بتوانم کاری بکنم...

مدت زیادی بود که هیچ حرکتی نکرده بودم. درست است، تکالیفم را انجام می‌دادم، اما آن فقط قدمی بود برای رسیدن به تکه‌کاغذی بی‌ارزش به نام دیپلم.

می‌خواستم کاری بکنم هرچند کوچک اما کاری که معنی داشته باشد، چیزی که اثری از من باقی بگذارد. چیزی خوبو همیشه به یاد داشته باشم که من انجامش داده‌ام. می‌دانستم شاید کمی خودخواهانه است، اما پیشانی‌ام را به در تکیه دادم، طرح چوب بلوط را با انگشت دنبال کردم و در حالی‌که چشمانم بسته بود، زیر لب زمزمه کردم: «تلاش کرده‌ای. شکست خورده‌ای. مهم نیست. دوباره تلاش کن. بهتر شکست بخور.»

لبخند زدم. مدّی پرسید: «مادرت این رو بهت گفته بود؟»

نمی‌توانستم نه بگویم، چون واقعاً درست بود و او می‌توانست ذهنم را بخواند. گفتم: «آره، این جمله واقعاً بهم امید می‌ده.»

منتظر بودم چیزی بگوید، اما دیدم مستقیم پشت سرم را نگاه می‌کند.

برگشتم و با شگفتی دیدم، درِ بلوطی باز شده بود.

فصل ۶

" چگونه آن کار را انجام دادی؟ "

مدّی با حیرت پرسید: «چگونه آن کار را انجام دادی؟» من شانه‌ام را بالا انداختم. من و مدّی آهسته به سمت درِ بلوطی رفتیم و برای اولین بار بعد از ساعتی گفت‌وگو و توضیح، از باغ قدم بیرون گذاشتیم.

با خودم فکر کردم: اگر من هم جزو آن گروهی باشم که قدرت دارند چه؟

فکرش خنده‌دار و کودکانه به نظر می‌رسید؛ مثل چیزی از کتابی پر از رنگین‌کمان، پری و جادو. مدّی که ذهنم را می‌خواند، گفت: «ممکنه کسی دیگه باعث شده باشه در خودش باز بشه؟» می‌دانستم او دارد در افکارم جست‌وجو می‌کند تا بفهمد چه شده. مدی گفت: «مایا، خودت در رو باز کردی، و تنها راه اینکه بفهمیم تو واقعاً جزو جامعه‌ی جادویی هستی اینه که...»

لحظه‌ای مکث کرد، سپس ناگهان پارچه‌ای بنفش و درخشان دور بدنم پیچید. با وحشت گفتم: «چه اتفاقی داره می‌افته؟!» مدّی در جواب من گفت: «این همان، پارچه جادویی و سحر آمیز است.اگر بعد از اینکه، پارچه

را از دور خودت برداری، شروع به پرواز کرد، به معنای آنست، تو جادوگری و اگر به زمین بیفتد تو فقط یک موجود معمولی و طبیعی هستی.»

پس از یک دقیقه، پارچه از دور بدن جدا شد و در کمال تعجب من، پارچه براق نه پرواز کرد نه روی زمین افتاد. در عوض، در حالت شناور، به رنگ زرد براق خیلی کمرنگ در آمد. مدّی گفت: «جالبه. این واکنش بسیارناذره.»

من با تعجب پرسیدم : «خوب، این چه معنی می‌دهد؟»

او با لحنی علمی و دقیق پاسخ داد: "کاملاً مطمئن نیستم، اما نشون می‌ده که تو یک موجود جادویی هستی و حتی از بیشتر افراد معمولی قدرتمندتری."

«اما در عین حال به معنای این نیز هست که تو می‌توانی هم جادوگر سیاه[1] را کنترل کنی و هم جادوی خالص[2] را. در بیشتر موارد، انسان می‌تواند انتخاب کند جزئی از شر یا خیر باشد. چون آن‌ها می‌توانند هر دو نوع را کنترل کنند. اما این توانایی بسیار نادر است.»

مدّی به‌صورتی بسیار علمی حرف می‌زد، انگار من پروژه آزمایشگاهی بسیار جالبی بودم. من در مورد دانش وی و این کشف عجیب او درباره خودم نفس در سینه‌ام حبس شد. آه کشیدم. نمی‌خواستم موجود خاص باشم. نمی‌خواستم "ویژه" باشم. به دست‌هایم که می‌لرزیدند خیره شدم. مدّی پشتم را طوری ماساژ داد که حس گرما به من دست داد. هرگز طی چهار ده سال عمرم، چنین حسی نداشتم.با وجود تمام عجیب بودنش، به شکل غریبی احساس قدردانی داشتم.

من در این زمان، یک دوست خوب و تعدادی خاطره بدست آوردم. که هرگز فراموش نخواهم کرد. و با اینکه هنوز همه چیز دردناک بود، او کم‌کم کرد تا قلبم را باز کنم، به شکلی که حتی تصورش را هم نمی‌کردم.

1- Witchcraft

2- Magic

فصل ۷

بنابراین، ظرف ساعت بعد یا. . . .

حدود یک ساعت فقط در رفت‌وآمد بودم، نمی‌دانستم از کجا باید شروع کنم؛ گاهی فقط غرق در فکر بودم، گاهی در اندوه. ناگهان صدای زمزمه‌ای آرام و مبهم را شنیدم که از دور می‌آمد... و نزدیک‌تر می‌شد... و نزدیک‌تر... و بعد، ناگهان، دختری شبح‌مانند ظاهر شد. به‌نظر می‌رسید تنها و ترسیده است. اما هرچه نزدیک‌تر می‌آمد، چهره‌اش تغییر می‌کرد، بزرگ‌تر، قدبلندتر، زیباتر می‌شد... تا جایی که در برابرمان دختری زیبا ایستاد با موهای قهوه‌ای براق و چشمان آبی درخشان.

او تقریباً شبیه...

مدی فریاد زد. «مامان!» مادرش دستش را به‌سوی او دراز کرد.

به نظر می‌رسید که آنها همدیگر را بغل کردند. او حتی مرا هم بغل کرد. اما متوجه شدم که چیزی پشت مرا به خارش انداخت. بغل گرفتن او خیلی آشنا بود، خنده‌اش، نرمی دستانش که بوی کرم مرطوب‌کننده می‌داد... همان‌گونه که مادر مدّی کم کم به‌شکل مادر من در می‌آمد، حس کردم احتیاج به نفس کشیدن دارم. اما نمی‌توانستم نفس بکشم. حس کردم انگار دارند روح مرا

می‌دزدند. می‌دانم احمقانه به نظر می‌آید.. اما نمی‌توانستم نفس بکشم. واکنش جنگ و گریز درونم فعال شد،و فکر می‌کنم چیزی میان هر دو را انتخاب کنم.

به سرعت گل روی درِ بلوطی را کندم و آن را جلوی صورتم گرفتم، انگار که داشتم بوسیله گل سپری در مقابل گلوله درست می‌کردم. مادرم ناگهان ایستاد، با نگاهی تیز به گل خیره شد و به همان سرعتی که آمده بود، در میان گلبرگ گل ناپدید شد.

ظاهراً مدّی تحت تأثیر قرار گرفته بود، اما در چهره‌اش چیزی بیشتر از تحسین دیده می‌شد، چیزی که پنهانش می‌کرد...

با عصبانیت در ذهنم گفتم:

لعنتی! ایکاش من هم می‌توانستم فکرش را بخوانم همانطور که او ذهن مرامی‌خواند!

و ناگهان، صدایی شبیه صدای مدّی در ذهنم طنین انداخت:

«چرا او داره با خشمش با مامانش می‌جنگد؟»

«ولی چقدر باهوش بود که ترفند گل نادر را به‌کار برد.»

«عجیبه که اون می‌تونه هم جادو و هم جادوگری تاریک رو کنترل کنه؛ نه خوبه نه بد.»

«حتماً مادرش هم قدرت هر دو رو داشته، برای همینه که احتمالاً همون مایرا بوده.»

«ولی چرا؟ مگه اون همراه خانواده‌ی مایا نمرده بود؟ خدایا، دلم براش می‌سوزه...»

چرا او این‌ها را فکر می‌کرد؟

اگر من نه جادو و نه جادوگری تاریک را انجام نمی‌دادم، پس چه بودم؟

دوباره من رانده و بی خانمان می‌شوم.

حتی در میان آن انسان‌های خاص و نادر؟

یا فقط... یک موجود عجیب؟

احساس خشم در درونم جوشید. ناگهان حس کردم دیگر نمی‌توانم به مدّی اعتماد کنم. اما باید می‌کردم، فعلاً.

به‌آرامی حس عجیبی از خشم درونم فوران کرد. نور شدیدی در چشمانم دوید، و بعد، همه چیز سیاه شد. سیاهِ مطلق. نه شناور بودم، نه در حال حرکت، فقط بالا و پایین می‌رفتم، مثل کسی که در تاریکی می‌جهد. ناگهان شکلی ترسناک ظاهر شد، شکلی به اندازه و شکل خودم، که حرکاتم را تقلید می‌کرد. فقط سایه‌ام بود.

در راهرویی صاف و بی‌پایان پیش می‌رفتم، در حالی که سایه‌ام جلوتر از من مانده بود. حرکتم را متوقف کرد. یخ زدم. سایه شروع به رشد کرد، بلند و بزرگ شد... بعد کوچک‌تر شد... و با وحشت دیدم که سایه به شکل مایرا درآمد.

ظاهرش کاملاً با آنچه قبلاً دیده بودم، متفاوت بود. مایرا خیلی تپل و چاق‌تر شده بود و زگیل‌های زیادی روی صورت بد شکل‌اش داشت. موهایش دیگر قهوه‌ای نبود، بلکه سبز-سیاه بود.

صدای شاعرانه مدّی در گوشم زنگ می‌زند: «آن‌ها کار جادوگراست.»

مدّی یواش به طرف من قدم زد و در نهایت شگفتی، به‌صورتم سیلی زد که شوربختانه ماشه خاطرات ترسناک را در ذهنم چکاند.

سوزش گونه‌ام را حس می‌کردم. صورتم را با دستانم گرفتم و به اطراف نگریستم و جلوی رویم زنی میانسال ایستاده بود با موهای قهوه‌ای، با

گونه‌های چاق، خط چشم و ماتیک قرمز براق، همراه با مژه مصنوعی چند لایه و برق لب براق. «مایا ویلو ارتگا، اصلاً بمن گوش می‌دهی؟!»

این صدای مادر عصبانی من بود. خیلی دلم برای مامانم تنگ شده بود، اما حالا من همه طعنه‌ها و حرف‌های او رابخاطرمی‌آورم. "کامل نیستی!" یا "بدترین دختر دنیایی!" با این حال هیچ‌وقت لبخندِ شیرین و دستان نرم و شفابخش او را فراموش نکردم. «مایا! آخ، تو هیچ‌وقت به‌من گوش نمی‌دهی، تو ای جوانک تهی‌مغز!» مادرم به‌سرعت طوفان به اتاقی دیگر رفت. به محض اینکه او رفت، خواهر کوچولوی من با نگاهی ترسناک وارد شد. او تمام مدت داشت به حرف‌های ما گوش می‌داد. سابرینا با غم بسیار در چشمانش پرسید: «مایا، مامان می‌خواهد ما را ترک کند؟ درست مثل بابا؟»

همگی ساکت بودند.

من با بغض، گفتم: «نه. البته که نه سابرینا.»

اشک در چشمانم حلقه زد. در همان حال درباره این فکر می‌کردم از سن ۸ سالگی چقدر خشم و اندوه در سینه نگه‌داشته‌ام بخاطر مَرد ابله و احمقی که در مورد خانواده‌اش بی‌فکر بود. اشک‌هایم را پاک کردم و سابرینا را محکم بغل کردم. ناگهان تمام نور ناپدید شد وحالا همه چیز تاریک بود.

من دوباره به راهروی تاریک برگشتم.

سابرینا داشت بزرگ می‌شد، قدش نیز بلندتر شده بود. سپس آستین پیراهن مرا گرفت و بخودش نزدیک‌تر کرد و با خشم گفت:

«چطور تونستی ما رو بیرون ماشین بذاری وقتی داشتن ما رو می‌کشتن؟!» معده‌ام ازحس گناه درد گرفت.

در حالی که سعی می‌کردم جلوی اشکم را بگیرم گفتم: «من واقعاً آن روز از دعوای خود با ایوی ناراحت و عصبانی بودم. نمی‌خواستم از ماشین پیاده شوم. نمی‌دانستم قراره همچین اتفاقی بیفته!»

سابرینا با سردی گفت: «تو دیگر خواهر من نیستی عشق من نسبت به تو در حال نابود شدنه!»

پیش از اینکه بتوانم حرف دیگری بزنم صدایی شنیده شد: «سابرینا، بیا اینجا. همین الان!» «بله مامان.» و سریع دوید.

من به جهتی که سابرینا می‌رفت نگاه کردم. سپس او به جهتی که من نگاه می‌کردم برگشت. من متوجه شدم که دارم مستقیم به صورت برادر بزرگترم توبی نگاه می‌کردم. او افسرده و غصه‌دار، اما جدی بود. پیش از اینکه با او تماس چشمی برقرار کنم، سریعاً نگاهم را دزدیدم. به زمین نگاه کردم. دیدم هیزل کنار پای توبی دراز کشیده بود. چرا هیزل اینجاست؟ همانطور که فکر می‌کردم، خم شدم و پشت گوش‌های او را نوازش کردم و موهای قهوه‌ای روشن و نرم او را لمس کردم.

هنگامی فهمیدم که خانواده‌ام در بهشت هستند و عملاً هیچگاه دوباره آن‌ها را نمی‌بینم، اشک بر پهنای صورتم، فرو ریخت.

همانطوری که هیزل را لمس و نوازش می‌کردم، توبی آنجا ایستاد انگار به سکوت راهرو گوش می‌دهد. توبی ناگهان با من ارتباط چشمی برقرار کرد و با نجوا گفت: «اون می‌خواد تو رو ببینه.» به او نگاه کردم. گیج بودم. من هم در جوابش به نجوا گفتم: «کی؟» توبی با سردی جواب داد: «دیگه کی می‌تونه باشه؟ مامان.»

ما از تاریکی عبور کردیم تا اینکه سر انجام به درِ چوبْ بلوطی رسیدیم. خیلی عجیب بود، ظاهراً شبیه دو درِ باغ‌های قبلی بود. این دَر، دقیقاً همان

تک‌گل کمیاب را هم داشت. گل نیلوفر آبی رنگی پروانشی زیبا با رگه‌های ریزسبز و آبی مواج. شگفت زده هستم، آیا مدّی می‌داند کجا هستم و حالم خوب است؟ اصلاً به این موضوع زیاد اهمیت می‌دهد؟ با احساس سوزانِ تازه در سینه، فکر کردم. توبی با لحنی که خیلی با حالت ریشخند و مسخره همیشگی او فرق داشت، گفت: "خوش بگذره." احساس کردم چقدر دلم برایش تنگ شده است. هیچ‌وقت خیلی نزدیک نبودیم تا بهترین خواهر و برادر باشیم. اما اوقات خوشی را با هم داشتیم. خنده‌های خوب.

با خودم گفتم، حالا وقتش است که از این موضوع رد شویم. از همه مهمتر، همه این‌ها یک خواب است که ظرف یک دقیقه با همه‌ی آدم‌های آن، محو خواهد شد و سرانجام من می‌توانم به برنامه‌ام برسم. ناگهان در، با سر و صدا باز شد و آن‌جا، داخل برج افسانه‌ای بلوطی مامانم ایستاده بود و داشت همه‌ی اطراف را نگاه می‌کرد. من خودم را در آیینه دیدم. درست مثل او نگاه می‌کردم.

برای لحظه‌ای، همه‌چیز را درباره واقعیت فراموش کردم که او واقعاً مامانم بود یا مایرا. اینکه او از جادو (و جادوگری) برای شیطان استفاده می‌کند یا اینکه هر گل بسیار نایاب را در تصرف دارد. کاملاً فراموش کردم. آن چه فکر می‌کردم قتل مادرم بود از همان لحظه‌ای که او را خون‌آلود بر زمین افتاده دیدم، اینک بی‌اندازه دلم برایش تنگ شده و مشتاق دیدارش بودم. تمامی باز گوی آن شب وحشتناک بود که زندگی مرا نابود کرد. مامان روی زمین افتاده بود. خون همه جا بود. خون... ترس... نگاه نگران او... آن نگاه هیچ‌گاه از چهره‌اش نرفت. چهره‌ای که بسیار دوست داشتم و همیشه دوست خواهم داشت.

هنگامی که دویدم تا او را تنگ در آغوش بگیرم، اشک روی گونه‌هایم سرازیر بود. به‌محض اینکه او را لمس کردم، او و تمامی محیط اطراف من، اتاق، راهروی تاریک ناپدید شد و در نور محو شد.

فصل ۸

نور مرا به بازگشت هدایت کرد.

نور مرا هدایت کرد تا به باغ برگردم. مدّی و هیزل دوان دوان بسوی من آمدند. مدّی پرسید: «خُب، تعریف کن چه اتفاقی افتاده؟» بر خلاف لحن پرسشش، عمیقاً نگران من بود. در میان گریه‌های بلند خود همه را تعریف کردم. از راهروی تاریک صاف تا دیدن توبی و مایا و این که چطوری مامانم را دیدم. مدّی واقعاً علاقمند بود که همه چیز را بداند. پس از اینکه همه چیز را برایش گفتم، مدّی اینطوری گفت: «خُب، وقتی رفته بودی، من به چیزی فکر کردم. چیزی بزرگ. خُب، خودت خوب می‌دانی، اگر مایرا شیشه جادویی قدرت خود را کاملاً پر می‌کرد، تو درباره آنچه رخ می‌داد، چه فکر می‌کردی؟»

سر تکان دادم. مدّی گفت: «بسته به آن دارد قدرت واقعاً چه چیز است، فکر می‌کنم اگر شیشه واقعاً پر است، در حرف، ما کاری نمی‌توانیم بکنیم. مایرا می‌تواند قلب و روح هر موجود جادویی را با استفاده از مایع سحرآمیز، بدزدد.» مدّی دیگر حرف نزد تا واکنش مرا ببیند. گوش می‌دادم، اما در عین حال فکرم جای دیگر بود.

آیا منظورش اینه آنچه که قبلاً با آن شبح اتفاق افتاده . . . یک نشانه بوده؟ طبیعی بود که مدّی این را شنیده و ناگهان ساکت شده باشد. «من فکر می‌کنم، ممکنه تو راست بگی. آن یک نشانه بود. یک پیام. مایا درست مثل

همان خواب هایی که می‌دیدی. مایرا مرتباً با تو تماس داشته و از وقتی که خانواده تو......... کشته شد، به تو نشانه‌ها و اشاره‌ها می‌داده. او ترا صدا می‌زده!»

و هنوز هم داشت تمام مدت مرا صدا می‌زد؟ آهسته با خودم فکر کردم. چرا این اتفاق‌ها برای من رخ می‌دهد؟ تمام چیزی که می‌خواهم این است که به تخت خوابم بروم و ساعت‌ها بخوابم تا وقتی که نور صبح بعدی از پنجره بتابد و بتوانم دوباره چهره‌ی سابرینا را در اتاق‌مان ببینم... اتاق قدیمی‌مان.

مدّی در حالی که همان لحظه طرح نقشه را از ذهنش می‌گذراند گفت: «خب، قدم اول: باید یاد بگیریم چطور آن آدم‌ها را دور هم جمع کنیم. قدم دوم: پیدا کردن مادرت و عمویت است. قدم سوم: پیدا کردن مایراست. و قدم چهارم: نجات دادن آدم‌های خاص از دست مایراست.»

با تردید گفتم: «گام چهارم به‌نظر می‌رسد، خودش چندین گام باشد.» ادامه دادم: «اما به هر صورت بیا جلو برویم.» چون ما بدون نقشه و آمادگی جلو می‌رویم.

و اینگونه به راه افتادیم؛ از میان باغ، از عمارت بیرونی، و به دل خیابان‌های تاریک و خالی زدیم.

و ما یک گروه غیر منتظره و عجیب: یک فرد سیزده ساله، یک نه ساله و یک سگ فانتزی طلایی.

فصل ۹

ما آنجا حداقل مدتی ایستادیم. . . . .

پس از این‌که خانه را ترک کردیم، حداقل ۱۵ دقیقه آنجا ایستاده بودیم. با بی‌قراری گفتم : «اصلاً از کجا باید شروع کنیم؟» مدّی با شک گفت: «حدس می‌زنم دور دنیا سفر کنیم؟» من با خودم گفتم: «باید راه بهتری هم باشه. . » آنگاه تمام دنیا به رنگ سبز درآمد. سبزِ تیره و عمیق، مثل رنگی زنده و پر رمزُ و راز.

چشمانم را باز کردم شاخه‌های درخت جلوی صورتم را گرفته بودند.

مدّی و هیزل پشت سرم ظاهر شدند. هر سه کاملاً گیج شده بودیم. چه اتفاقی افتاده بود؟

ظاهراً، ما، در باغ دیگری بودیم که درست مثل باغ خودمان بود، اما بجای درِ چوب بلوطی، دری از چوبِ درخت سروِ سرخ بود، با همان گلِ نادر و همان جزئیات دیگر. به سمتِ چپِ خود نگاه کردم، درست همان‌جا یک خانه عظیم، در کنارِ یک باغ، قرار گرفته بود. این همه چیز را برای واضح و آشکار کرد. مدّی لبخند زنان گفت: « غیر ممکنه!» من در دلم گفتم: «اتفاقاً ممکنه!»

انگار که من گروهمان را به خانه‌ی یکی از افراد خاص و قدرتمند آورده بودم، از آن افراد داری قدرت که باغِ سّریِ خودشان، را دارند.

پرسیدم: «صبر کنید، پس این بدان معناست که مردمانی که ما آنان را خاص می‌دانیم، همگی یک باغ اسرارآمیز درخانه خود دارند؟ شخصی که خانه‌ها را می‌سازد، آیا می‌داند مالک بعدی، یکی از آنها خواهد بود؟» مدّی سریع جواب داد: «نه، اینطور، فکر نمی‌کنم، فکر کنم باغِ مخفی و اسرارآمیز، فقط یک نشونه است، یک نشانه که تو یکی از آنها هستی و فقط به هر خانه‌ای که بروی با تو جا به جا می‌شود و همراهت می‌مونه.» بعد ادامه داد: «همین طور، مایا....، آشکارا منظورم این است که تو، مانند همه‌ی ما خاص هستی، حتی قدرت و نیروی تو نیز خاص‌تر است. تو می‌توانی با آرزو کردن چیزی رو واقعی کنی.. . اوه صبر کن، امیدوارم که اصلاً به چیزهای بد فکر نکرده باشی، ولی خلاصه....، فقط مواظب باش.»

مواظب باش.

عبارتی که در طول زندگی‌ام بیش از اندازه شنیده‌ام، و حالا دیگر به‌نظر نمی‌رسد واقعاً ممکن باشد.

فصل ۱۰

ما کمی آنجا ایستادیم و فقط به باغ مخفی یکی از همنوعانمان خیره شدیم
. . . . باغ مخفی و سحرآمیزِ همان افراد داری قدرت خاص. او احتمالاً
حتی خودش نمی‌دانست که باغی آنجاست. حدود پنج دقیقه طول کشید
تا بالاخره آرام به‌سوی درِ بلوطی باغشان قدم برداشتم. مدّی پشت سرم
می‌آمد. در را باز کردم، ترسان بودم که دوباره همان اتفاق قبلی تکرار شود،
یعنی جایی که نور مرا کور کرده بود.

و دقیقاً همان اتفاق افتاد. اما این‌بار چیزی غیرمنتظره روی داد. من احساس
کردم جایی معلقم، در حالی‌که آرام، خیلی آرام، به سمت پایین فرو می‌رفتم،
هیزل را در آغوش گرفته بودم. مثل اینکه در حال سقوط بودم، اما آهسته،
بی‌وزن و آرام. مدّی هم این بار کنارم بود.

پرتو سبز ضعیفی زیر پای ما وجود داشت، و به‌سمتش پایین می‌رفتیم. ناگهان
با صدای تالاب فرود آمدیم. در دنیای دیگری بودیم، دنیایی پوشیده از
چمن. مدّی از جایش بلند شد، اما همان لحظه دوباره به زمین افتاد. من هم

ناگهان حس عجیبی مثل سوزش در خود احساس کردم. دماغم با بوهای دود آلود زیاد پر شد و خیلی زود خسته شدم و در چمن ولو شدم.

آخرین چیزی که بخاطر می‌آورم دیدن دختری سراپا خون‌آلود بود که بالای سرم ایستاده بود و مستقیم به چشمانم، می‌نگریست. چشمان آبی و یخ زده‌اش او بطور غریبی به روحم خیره شده بود، که انگار خون در رگ‌هایم یخ زد و دوباره عالم سیاه شده.

دوباره.

فصل ۱۱

و چیزی مانند این رخ داده بود . . . . . .

چیزی مانند این قبلاً برای من پیش آمده بود.

وقتی که ۸ ساله بودم.

یک روز بعد از روزی بود که پدرم تَرکمان کرد.آن روز نباید آن‌طور گریه می‌کردم. چون او هرگز پدر واقعی من نبود، فقط پدر **بی‌احساس** من بود.

اما من گریه کردم. آن‌قدر زیاد گریه کردم، که غش کردم و دنیا دوباره، ساعت‌ها سیاه شد. چند بار چشمانم را باز کردم، اما تاریکی به من احساس آرامش می‌داد. تاریکی حواسم را از درد پرت می‌کرد. آن‌قدر مدت طولانی در تخت ماندم که همه نگرانم شدند.اما هیچ‌کس به مادرم فکر نکرد. چون مامانم کسی بود که به پدرم اهمیت می‌داد. همه سال‌هائی که با او زندگی کرده بود.

و آنوقت پدرم به همین سادگی رهایش کرد.

تقریباً بعد از سه روز تمام، من از تختخواب بیرون آمدم. من هرگز خشم روی صورت مامانم را فراموش نخواهم کرد.

گیج از خواب بیدار شدم. دنیا تار و مبهم بود، اما کم کم شکل گرفت. همه جا تار بود و نفسم بریده بریده و لرزان بود.

بوی زننده گل‌ها چنان آزاردهنده بود که تا مرز بی‌حالی پیش رفتم. مدّی کنارم نیمه هشیار از خواب برخاست. حس کردم در کُمُدی پر از گیاه در تله افتاده‌ام. تلاش کردم بنشینم، اما سریع با پشت روی چمن افتادم، پلک چشم‌هایم سنگین بود، دنیا تاریک‌تر می‌شد.

در همان حال، دنیا دوباره در تاریکی فرو رفت، چشمانم سنگین شدند، در حالی‌که می‌ترسیدم شاید دیگر بازشان نکنم.

فصل ۱۲

دنیا صاف نبود. . . . . .

دنیا مه‌آلود و تار بود. من هنوز مدهوش، روی چمن، افتاده بودم، اما کم‌کم می‌توانستم شکل‌هایی را تشخیص دهم.

پیکری بلند بالای سرم ایستاد. گفت: «فراموش نکن. سرانجام همه بتو پشت خواهند کرد. حتی خودت. تو اویی مایا. اویی، او. خودت می‌دانی. حتی سعی نکن که آنرا انکار کنی.»

با احساسی از سردرگمی و شکست در قلبم بیدار شدم. چه مدت بی‌هوش بوده‌ام؟ مدّی خوبه؟ هنوز هم اینجاست؟

ناگهان، همه چیز برای مدت حدود کسرِ ثانیه، تاریک و سیاه شد، پیش از این که بانوئی بلند قامت در برابر ظاهر شود. و بعد زنی بلندقد جلویم ظاهر شد. سریع از جا برخاستم، آماده فرار.

او با صدای عمیق و مرموز گفت: «هی، خودتی؟» خیلی گیج شدم. خودم هستم؟ یعنی چی؟

ابروهایم تا مرز موهایم بالا رفت وقتی فهمیدم «یعنی تو منی؟ از آینده؟» او با لحنی سرزنش‌آمیز و مغرور گفت:

«آه، این‌قدر بچه‌گانه حرف نزن دختر جوان. البته که بله، من تو هستم. ببین، این اتفاقی که افتاده، از لحظه‌ای که خانواده‌ات کشته شدند، باعث شد... چطور بگویم... یک شکاف در جهان ایجاد شود.

چون، خب، جهان متوجه شد چیزی در ذهنت قرار گرفته که تمام آینده‌ات را آشکار می‌کند. تمام رؤیاها و "تصاویر ذهنی"ای که در این ۳۶۸ روز گذشته دیدی، به‌اضافه‌ی روزهایی که در این دنیای عجیب و تازه سپری کردی، همه نشانه بودند. می‌فهمی؟

عالی، پس بگذار ادامه بدهم. و حالا من این‌جا هستم تا آینده‌ات را برایت فاش کنم، چون دیر یا زود، وقتی برای متوقف کردن من می‌آمدی، خودت آن را کشف می‌کردی.»

با ترس گفتم: «صبر کن، تو... مایرا هستی؟»

و ناگهان همه‌چیز برایم معنا پیدا کرد. آخرین حرف‌های مادرم... آخرین تصویری که دیده بودم...و فهمیدم تمام آن مایراهایی که در رؤیاهایم دیده بودم، هیچ‌کدام مادرم نبودند.

همه‌شان من بودم. من همان دختر شیطانی‌ام. چیزی درونم پیچید، انگار پازلی در جای خود قرار می‌گرفت. آسمان همیشه خاکستری حالا آبیِ عمیقی شد. شکاف جهان در حال ترمیم بود اما زخم درون من نه.

و هرگز نخواهد بود. فهمیدم سرنوشت من چیست. من در نهایت قاتل می‌شوم.

بخشِ پایانی

خوب. پس داستان را تا اینجا خواندید، بی‌فایده‌ترین قصه شخص نجات یافته و باز مانده‌ای که تا به حال گفته شده است. و با وجود این، اگر هنوز می‌خوانید، این بدان معناست که قصه به نحوی برای شما جالب بوده است. و این واقعاً، عالی است. شما را ستایش می‌کنم که دارید مرا درک می‌کنید که سزاوار آن هستم، اما کمی فکر کن...

دوست داشتنِ دردِ این روایت چه چیزی درباره‌ی تو می‌گوید، هان؟ از خواندنِ تراژدی‌هایی که در ذهنم می‌گذرد لذت می‌بری؟

آن درد درون من، با تمام سوزندگی‌اش، چیزی‌ست که باید با آن زندگی کنم.

این، فقط زندگی من است.

دست کم ممکن است، شاید من هنوز بهترین زن اون بیرون باشم. من دست کم، کاری انجام دادم. هر چند عجیب. شاید بالاخره در چیزی بهترین شده‌ام. حداقل شاید این زخم، دیر یا زود، درمان شود.

خوشحالم که حتی در این خیالِ فریبنده زندگی می‌کنم، چون در اعماق وجودم می‌دانم که آن زخم هرگز درمان نخواهد شد. همیشه آن‌جا خواهد بود، می‌سوزد، می‌جوشد، در قلبم می‌چرخد، و با یاد گذشته آرامم می‌دهد. گاهی درد آن‌قدر غیرقابل‌تحمل می‌شد که در خیال، به کودکی‌ام پناه می‌بردم،

به روزهایی که در دشت‌ها می‌دویدم، آفتاب بر صورتم می‌تابید، راه‌ها باز و بی‌انتها بودند. می‌دویدم و می‌دویدم، بی‌آن‌که چیزی از دنیا بدانم، چون هنوز دنیا به من آسیب نزده بود.

آن خاطرات برایم معنیِ آزادی بودند... تا زمانی که به بخشی از خاطرات می‌رسیدم که زندگی‌ام سراشیب سقوط را آغاز کرد.

آن روز لعنتی...

آن روزِ احمقانه و لعنتی.

و وقتی دوباره شروع به رؤیا دیدن می‌کردم، دیگر نمی‌توانستم متوقفش کنم. آن رؤیا را خیلی واضح به یاد دارم، پشت درِ ماشین پنهان شده بودم، باد به صورتم می‌وزید.

با خودم فکر کردم: «به‌زودی باران می‌گیرد.» بلند شدم تا گوشی‌ام را از روی آسفالت بردارم، همان گوشی که چند متر دورتر پرت شده بود. من رسیدم و رسیدم، انگشتان من لبه صفحه را لمس می‌کرد خیلی نزدیک بودِ که تلفن را چنگ بزند و شماره کسی را بگیرد و به کسی زنگ بزند، هرکسی که باشد. اما ناگهان صدای تیز و خشنی شنیدم، صدای چاقویی که هوا را می‌شکافت و روی زمین، درست جلوی صورتم افتاد.

آهسته ایستادم، به این امید که هر چه آهسته‌تر برخیزم، او زودتر ناپدید شود.
اما نشد.
او ماند.
در ذهنم.
و همیشه می‌ماند، تا پایانِ وجودم.

دیگر نمی‌توانم این را «زندگی» بنامم، وقتی تمامش صرفِ مرورِ گذشته می‌شود، بارها و بارها...

می‌دانم دارم دوباره پرحرفی می‌کنم، اما نمی‌توانم جلوِ خودم را بگیرم، همان‌طور که آن روز نتوانستم از مادرم، سابرینا، و توبی محافظت کنم...

در آن روز احمقانه و لعنتی. آیا آن‌ها فقط رؤیا بودند؟ با اضطراب از خودم می‌پرسم، چرا دیگر چهره‌شان را به‌خوبی به یاد نمی‌آورم؟

اما هنوز می‌توانم صدای خنده‌اش را بشنوم، آن خنده‌ی مرگبار و هولناک. سرد و یخ‌زده، مثل چشمانی که وقتی روبه‌رویش ایستادم نمی‌توانستم از نگاهشان فرار کنم. نمی‌دانم چرا این‌طورم. نمی‌دانم هدفش چیست.

نمی‌دانم چرا احساس می‌کنم در خوابی بی‌پایانم.

خوابی بی‌پایان، اما پر از درد.

آه، چه دردناک. می‌سوزد. و این سوختن... تمام نمی‌شود. نمی‌دانم باید چه کنم. نمی‌دانم... کی دوباره بیدار خواهم شد.

با وحشت از خواب پریدم. عرق از صورتم سرازیر بود و در چشمان خسته‌ام جمع می‌شد. سردرگم بودم، چون مطمئن بودم این رؤیا را قبلاً هم دیده‌ام.

پایان.

Aknowledgments

The biggest thanks I have to give right now is to Kidsocado for having an advertisement at a fashion event where they helped me finally achieve my dream (since I was 9) of publishing a book! I also greatly thank Ms. King who was my grade 5 teacher, I love writing and she really made me feel like I was good at what I like to do. So, thank you for making us write creepy stories (even though this didn't turn out to be the spooky version) on October 30th, 2020.

Because I would've never written this book.

قدردانی

در اینجا، باید بیشترین مراتب سپاسگزاری خود از انتشارات کیدزوکادو بکنم بابت غرفه‌ی که در یک نمایشگاه مد در ونکوور داشتند و باعث آشنایی من با آنها شد و باعث شد سرانجام رویایی که از سن ۹ سالگی برای انتشار یک کتاب داشتم تحقق پیدا کند.

همچنین از خانم کینگ، معلم کلاس پنجمم، از صمیم قلب سپاسگزارم. من عاشق نوشتنم، و او باعث شد باور کنم در کاری که دوست دارم، واقعاً خوبم. پس متشکرم که ما را واداشتید داستان‌های ترسناک بنویسیم (هرچند این یکی در نهایت ترسناک از آب درنیامد!) در تاریخ ۳۰ اکتبر ۲۰۲۰، چون اگر آن روز نبود، شاید هرگز این کتاب نوشته نمی‌شد.

پایان

The story you have just read is more than an engaging mystery—it is the result of a beautiful collaboration between a granddaughter and her grandfather. Shaya wrote the original story in English, and her grandfather translated it with great care and affection. This intergenerational partnership has breathed new life into the book and made it even more special.

داستان پیشِ رو تنها یک ماجرای اسرارآمیز جذاب نیست؛ ثمره‌ی همکاری زیبای یک نوه و پدربزرگ است. شایا آن را به انگلیسی نوشت و پدربزرگش با عشق ترجمه‌اش کرد. همین همراهی دو نسل، روح تازه‌ای به این کتاب بخشیده است.

Author Biography

Shaya Motamedi is an Iranian-Candian grade 10 student, who wrote this book when she was in grade 6, She has had a love for writing since she was in the third grade.

She enjoys reading horror & thriller novels. Her other passions include being on her school's basketball team and playing the piano. Shaya currently lives with her family in Vancouver, British Columbia located in southwest of Canada.

The Garden of Magic and Witchcraft is her first published book, initially written when she was eleven years old.

Translator Biography

Mohammad A. Atashbarg, born in Yazd,Iran in 1948, is a passionate writer and translator.

His first short story was published while he was still in high school. He earned his M.A. as a top graduate from the Faculty of Law and Political Science at the University of Tehran, and later pursued three years of graduate studies at Loyola University of Chicago.

Over the years, he has been author or co-author of few translated books and has written nearly fifty articles across various fields, including international law and international relations,social issues and satire.

Today, as a proud grandfather, he's translating a book written by his teenage granddaughter—continuing his lifelong dedication to language and learning.

درباره‌ی شایا

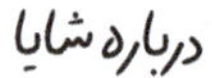

شایا معتمدی یک دانش‌آموز ایرانی-کانادایی است که از دوران کلاس سوم دبستان عاشق نوشتن بوده است او از خواندن رمان‌های ترسناک و هیجان‌انگیز لذت می‌برد. دیگر علایقش شامل حضور در تیم بسکتبال مدرسه و نواختن پیانو است.

شایا در حال حاضر به همراه خانواده‌اش در شهر ونکوور، در استان بریتیش کلمبیا، واقع در جنوب غربی کانادا زندگی می‌کند.

کتاب The Garden of Magic and Witchcraft نخستین اثر منتشر شده‌ی اوست، که نگارشش را در یازده سالگی آغاز کرده بود و یک سال بعد توسط پدر بزرگ شایا محمد آتش برگ ترجمه شد به نام باغ جادو و جادوگر که اکنون در دستان شماست.

درباره‌ی محمد

م. ع. آتش بَرگ، متولد ۱۳۲۷ در یزد، فارغ‌التحصیل فوق‌لیسانس از دانشکده حقوق و علوم سیاسی دانشگاه تهران و دارای تجربه سه سال تحصیلات تکمیلی در دانشگاه لایولای شیکاگو است. او همواره دلبسته و پرشور در زمینه نویسندگی و ترجمه بوده و نخستین داستان کوتاهش را در دوران دبیرستان به چاپ رسانده است.

تاکنون بیش از ۵۰ مقاله و چندین کتاب به زبان‌های فارسی و انگلیسی از او در حوزه‌های حقوق، روابط بین‌الملل، مسائل اجتماعی، داستان کوتاه و طنز منتشر شده است.

اکنون، در مقام یک پدربزرگ، مترجم کتاب داستانی است که نوه نوجوانش نوشته است!

End of the English Section